Zoe: An Act In Two Plays

La Lisière de la forêt [Treeline]

Only Stupid Birds Sing

Gregory Ferris

La Lisière de la forêt

[Treeline]

A play in 2 acts

By Gregory Ferris

CHARACTERS

Charles

French, long time criminal who has never been arrested. Living in the US for less than 3 years. Resides with his girlfriend Zoe in a small rural community of psychics and spiritualists in Rose Hill in central Pennsylvania. Maintains a low profile while running an illicit busines. Enjoys walks in the nearby forests and watching birds of prey.

Zoe

French, much younger companion of Charles and, as a very effective, but undisclosed medium, assists with his enterprise. She is seeking a normal life without Charles.

Arthur

American, middle aged, widower, sheriff. Long time law enforcement, who has found a pleasant niche in the town of Rose Hill. Has a very easy going manner, but has much experience with real criminals. Very attuned to the needs of policing in a small town, where odd is normal, and where the tourists outnumber the residents. Carries his revolver hidden in order to not appear threatening. Enjoys finer things in life, and has a working knowledge of French.

Buck

Youngish son of Sheriff Arthur. Sole proprietor of a small logging company that contracts with an out of state baseball bat manufacturer. Enjoys bird watching and nature, and sees his vocation as managing the forest with its inhabitants, i.e. animals and the tree spirits, the latter whom he knows by name. Romantically interested in Zoe. Shares Charles' interest in bird watching. Neither sophisticated nor a rustic.

Madame Crystal	Chris Burns, American. Recent arrival to Rose Hill. Originally from Chicago, she used to teach French, but now supports herself as Madame Crystal, a Hungarian Psychic, not a medium. Attracted to strong, confident men, to counterbalance the many clients that she sees as needy and weak. Has a true gift. She pursues both Arthur, and, more recently Charles.
Irma Leek	Middle aged medium, longtime resident of Rose Hill, girlfriend of Arthur
Offstage voices	

SETTING

Town Square in Rose Hill, Charles' and Zoe's residence,
Madame Crystal's practice and the Sheriff's office.
Summer 1992

Act I scene 1 town square, day 1 mid morning
Act I scene 2 home of Zoe and Charles, day 2 early morning
Act I scene 3 home of Madame Crystal, day 2 late morning
Act I scene 4 home of Madame Crystal, day 2 noon.
Act I scene 5 town squarea, day 2 later in the afternoon

Act II scene 1 Sheriff's office, day 3 afternoon
Act II scene 2 Sheriff's office, day 3 continuing
Act II scene 3 Town Square, day 4 mid morning

ACT I

SCENE 1

(*Town square of Rose Hill, voices of crowd and "performers" will be heard off stage, with commentary by characters on stage, light, happy music until the readings begin*)

CHARLES

Ces séances publiques sont trop drôles. Un véritable cirque. Qu'en penses-tu Arthur?

ARTHUR

Je suis d'accord, Charles. It is quite a circus. Even without these public readings, Rose Hill is still a circus.

CHARLES

(*Smiling*) Fewer ballons is the only difference. These events recall to me your western movies with their scenes of public hangings. The same anticipation and festive atmosphere.

ARTHUR

There is a festive atmosphere, sure. You can see that with the teeshirts and the newly purchased Rose Hill ball caps. It still has a touch of solemnity. But it's a different anticipation. It's true of any spectacle. I very much doubt that anyone here is expecting a hanging or any type of killing. An unnatural death in tiny Rose Hill would really mess up my week. Heck, it would "kill" my perfect record here.

CHARLES

It's a great irony that no one is ever murdered in the village of the dead.

ARTHUR

Like a cemetery.

CHARLES

Zoe says the same as you. She compares this town to a cemetery as well.

ARTHUR

She must be suffocating here. She is only what, 21 22?

CHARLES

Probably.

ARTHUR

Probably? You don't know how old she is?

CHARLES

The crowd is growing anxious. It's not an expectation of death that I sense at these readings, but an elevated level of suspense. The crowd needs a resolution, it needs to have an answer to the meaning of existence.

ARTHUR

Hah! The meaning of existence, you say. I suspect that the more agitated ones simply want to know if the dearly departed left them a hidden treasure, and, if so, where it is buried. The meaning of existence? I wish them good luck with that.

CHARLES

Mais oui. Knowledge is a hidden treasure as well.

ARTHUR

And they expect to receive either of those treasures here in a hick town on a sunny July morning?

CHARLES

Why not? This hick town is the capital of strange. I tell friends back in Paris that it is the Dodge City of the unusual.

ARTHUR

You must have seen too many spaghetti westerns as a young man, Dodge City of the strange. That's a good one.

Given that many of these spiritual treasure hunters return to Rose Hill again and again, it seems that they have not found any answer at all. For some it may be a pilgrimage. I concede any argument on philosophy to you Charles, you French excel at that. I could never even pronounce the name of your French philosopher, Sartre correctly, let alone understand his ideas. I used to carry a copy of his book to impress prospective girlfriends.

CHARLES

So did I.

ARTHUR

Did it work for you?

CHARLES

No, not often.

ARTHUR

Me neither. It seemed that every other young guy was carrying a copy. Sartre flooded the casual dating market.

CHARLES

I don't believe that was his motive.

ARTHUR

I switched to carrying that Chinese guy's book.

CHARLES

Mao's little red book?

ARTHUR

That's the one.

CHARLES

Did you have better success with it?

ARTHUR

Somewhat. At least is was easier to port around. Plus, I could slide it into my pocket if I wasn't interested in the girl.   Sartre's was just too heavy, I couldn't hide it in an emergency.

CHARLES

Emergency?

ARTHUR

You know, if the girl was maybe a philosophy major. It wouldn't work if she knew more than I did about Sartre.

CHARLES

That makes sense in an odd way.

ARTHUR

o be honest, I didn't understand what he was saying, but he took a very long time to say it.

CHARLES

His ideas are too important to be understood.

ARTHUR

Too important to be understood. Is that supposed to make sense? What in the world does that even mean?

CHARLES

That, in essence, humanity must believe lies in order to survive.

ARTHUR

Sartre said that?

CHARLES

No, I did. He is just one example of my statement. His writings provided millions of admirers with a credible lie. Or at least a credible hypothesis.

ARTHUR
I'd have to think about that, Charles.

CHARLES
Look around at the people here. Isn't it clear that they are here in search of truth, which is another name for a credible lie?

ARTHUR
I think that you give too much credit to humans. I'd bet that some of the young men in the crowd see Rose Hill as the two of us saw Sartre, as a means to an end, in bed. They are looking for their own version of heaven on earth.

CHARLES
Perhaps a few of them are, not all. The hanging crowd in your cowboy films wonders if it will observe the soul of the hanged depart like a vapor from the body; today's audiences wonders if the soul of the departed is still "hanging around", as you say.

Il s'agit de transition, a matter of transition, the crossing over. Here, we live surrounded by thousands and thousands of hectares of trees, interspersed with open fields and farmland.

ARTHUR
And smack in the middle is this oasis, Rose Hill.

CHARLES
There is a transition between forest and field, an edge, une lisière.

Don't you sometimes wonder if a person can provide startling insights, the closer they are to this lisière de la forêt, this treeline, the edge between life and death? The westerns ask it of those who are about to leave this forest, those about to be hung. Today's visitors to our small oasis ask it of those who have passed beyond the treeline of the living. Do the dearly departed have any guidance for the living?

ARTHUR

Wow. In addition to philosophy, I've made a note not to compete with you in poetry either, Charles. It's about to be hanged.

CHARLES

Pardon?

ARTHUR

It's about to be hanged, not about to be hung.

CHARLES

English grammar is confusing.

ARTHUR

It's a good thing for this town that I double as a grammar policeman.

CHARLES

There is no such thing, you are joking again.

ARTHUR

I am. But the word is hanged.

In your beloved westerns, Clint Eastwood usually just spits tobacco after the trap door of the scaffold has sprung. And then he and his horse ride on. That, I understand. You live, you work, and then you die. Simple.

I leave the big picture view to those who enjoy it. I am just a small thinking, small town cop.

CHARLES

You should have those words engraved on your badge.

ARTHUR

You mentioned believing lies in order to survive. You may be right. I'm not sophisticated.

CHARLES

Yes you are. Just in an American way.

ARTHUR

(*side glance*) Hmmm.

CHARLES

People crave puzzles, but puzzles are considered boring if there is no answer. It does not make sense, but it's true. Humans are weird.

ARTHUR

You're telling me. Weird they are. I enjoy slices of the weird, they're like slice of cold black raspberry pie. The occasional eccentricity can be fun. Many of the criminals that I've chased and captured were eccentric.

CHARLES

So are police. Did you ever consider that you only ever caught the stupid ones (*pause*) and the very smart ones, those that you classify as eccentric?

ARTHUR

Meaning what? I captured enough bad guys, more than my share. I did my part and it isn't bragging. I still catch one, now and again. I'm more selective, like a trophy hunter, at this point in my career.

CHARLES

Meaning that the above average criminal, the bourgeois crminal successfully eluded you.

ARTHUR

I've never met a bourgeois; is that a country in South America? (*pause*) Hmmm, you may be right. So it follows that their crimes are bourgeois, not a graphic murder or large scale embezzlement or theft?

CHARLES

Those sorts of crimes were all likely highly visible, with a limited and sometimes obvious pool of suspects.

ARTHUR
You evidently watch lots of British murder mysteries. Between westerns and Agatha Christie, you must see crime and violence as commonplace, occurring everywhere and all the time. This is simply not reality; it may be yours, but it's not mine. I find the British stories are too complex, with shallow characters and contrived plots.

CHARLES
I've noticed that also. Nevertheless, the world can be dangerous.

ARTHUR
Then you chose well in hiding yourself away here, I keep this town safe.

CHARLES
But who will protect me from you?

ARTHUR
Me?

CHARLES
Sometimes the British inspector is the villain. At least in the movies.

ARTHUR
I'm not British. You can trust the American police. Anyway, I prefer the French, or rather Belgian detective mystery series of Maigret to any British author. That author, Georges something or other, addressed the why of crime, and didn't confuse either himself or the reader with intricate details of who and how. The why of human behavior is always the most difficult puzzle to solve.

CHARLES
And not the who? You arrested people, not motives.

ARTHUR
One leads to the other. Often time finding a why leads directly to discovering the who. (*pause*) Everyone is guilty of something. (*pause*) This country would be better off if everyone spent 3-6 months in prison.

CHARLES

You are joking yet again.

ARTHUR

Not entirely. France has universal military service, right?

CHARLES

Yes, as do many countries.

ARTHUR

I think that deep down, maybe subconsciously, that countries do this in order to demonstrate how dreary and terrible military life can be, even in peacetime. This in turn deters war.

CHARLES

So military training deters war?

ARTHUR

Yes. And the same could be done by us, the police, for crime. If we had universal penal service then we could deter first time offenders.

CHARLES

You would put the entire population in prison?

ARTHUR

Sure, it makes perfect sense. Not all at once, that would be too difficult and disruptive, and it wouldn't be permanent. Just a few months for every citizen, and immigrants, of course. It would be fair to everyone.

CHARLES

I might prefer a British inspector after all.

ARTHUR

Getting back to your point about the criminals that I have imprisoned in the past. Are you suggesting that it only requires an average mind to conceive of a master crime, that it to say, a crime that goes unseen ? Is that your hypothesis? Or is that only a credible lie?

CHARLES

Some of both. But what do I know of this Arthur, I'm just a mostly retired businessman and bird watcher.

ARTHUR

Average?

CHARLES

(*Laughs*) Yes, average. I prefer retired. And you, Arthur, have you thought more of retirement?

ARTHUR

Yes, I have. But I'm still not sure. This job is semi-retirement as it is. That is why I took it, after all.

CHARLES

And to be near to you son.

ARTHUR

Yes, that too. He's an odd one. I thought that he'd outgrow his "condition", but he's grown into it. Buck does ok, whether it's because of his "gift" or despite it, I haven't been able to determine. Either way, he is building a solid career and a successful business.

CHARLES

And your own career, is that ending? You were hired as sheriff because you possessed skills that you no longer need to use.

ARTHUR

Perhaps not all of them. I still know how to protect a Podunk town.

CHARLES

Is that a disappointment to you?

ARTHUR

No, it's not disappointing at all. I have no desire to either police in or live in a town where I hear gunshots at all hours of the day and night.

CHARLES

Except for the local hunters.

ARTHUR

Yes, except for them.

CHARLES

And the poachers.

ARTHUR

Neither of them concern me. That's work for the game warden.

CHARLES

And the local women?

ARTHUR

I don't want them shooting anyone either.

CHARLES

What? Oh, another American joke. What do you think of these local women? Are you friends with any of them?

ARTHUR

All of my friends are one drink women.

CHARLES

(*Drumroll offstage*) Does that include Irma? (*pointing offstage*)

IRMA

My name is Irma Leek. I'm here with you on this beautiful July morning to conduct a public séance. The callers who contact me from the other side do so of their own volition. You must all be patient.

It can be difficult, especially with a group of this size, thanks to all you for coming I must say. It can be difficult to contact one specific soul.

So, if you need, or want, private attention, please contact either myself or one of the other mediums afterward. Each of the mediums and psychics has a small sign in their yard listing their hours and phone number, and whether they accept wallkins or only scheduled appointments.

So, let's begin, and see what, and who, we have today.

(*drumroll*) Thanks for the drum roll, Patrick. It helps to lower the tension. (*laughs*) Folks, this is a friendly séance. Think of it as a tailgate party, or a family reunion. We don't stand on formality. You too have a part to play, this is an interactive process.

We won't have any bumps in the night, since we're gathered in the middle of glorious summer day.

Oh, we are in luck; our first spirit is here with us now.

I am sensing, a Robert in the crowd, no not Robert, but Robbie. Your uncle passed a while back, several months at least. He and you, I'm sensing, feeling a W, a William or Willard.

VOICE

My uncle Willie.

IRMA

Yes. Uncle Willie. He mentions fishing with you, how much he enjoyed it

VOICE

That's right. He taught me how to fish.

IRMA

And to exaggerate, Willie says. He's wearing a very odd hat, its not what fishermen typically wear. He is quite noticeable with it on his head. It have a very wide brim, very broad. Why, it's a sombrero.

VOICE

That's my uncle.

IRMA

Why the sombrero, Willie? Willie won't say. He just tipped his sombrero and indicates that he wants Robbie to respond instead.

VOICE

He used it to measure his catch. It was a double hatter, or a half hatter, stuff like that. That was just his little joke.

IRMA

I see. A mad hatter you might say. He says to fish as much as you can and to remember him. He is leaving now; he certainly seems content. I'm not sure if he is going fish there now or not. If he was a true fisherman, he certainly won't tell a crowd of this size where the best holes may be found, either here or over there.

He may not be fishing, but in a way, I am, so I am going to release Willie now and see if who else from over there wants to contact someone in this audience.

Oh, I'm sorry, everyone. In advance, I apologize. This spirit is very insistent. She hasn't learned patience, I'm afraid that she hasn't really had time to learn anything. But this is important, she matters. I find this sad, I am very sorry, but I have to do this now. Spirits contact me by themselves, it can be all jumbled and confusing, a rush of voices and images. Like Black Friday shopping. Crowds over there and ones over here.

I have a very sweet young person here with me, she is very young, one could say regrettably that she hardly even lived. She is calling for her mother. She is too young to even know her own name, but she is calling for mama.

(*Scream from woman in the crowd*)

FEMALE VOICE

Oh Meghan, Meghan, Meghan. Oh no. Oh Meghan.

IRMA

I am so sorry ma'am did you lose a baby in childbirth?

SAME FEMALE VOICE

Tell Meghan that "mama loves you". Oh Meghan.

IRMA

She knows ma'am, she knows. Meghan is content and will wait for you. She has learned love. That is enough.

CHARLES

Why does Irma do that? She could have ignored the child, or done it more privately.

ARTHUR

It is not her way.

CHARLES

But so young.

ARTHUR

Irma doesn't avoid giving her client's pain. She must be convinced that it helps. (*pause*)

How can that be good for the living? It can't be. It's cruel. (*pause*). She obviously disagrees with me. She is the professional. Its her line of work. I guess that it is good for business. (*pause*)

CHARLES

So young.

ARTHUR

Zoe is too young for you.

CHARLES

What? (*pause*) Everyone always asks me about Zoe. You, all of you, are so curious. She must be the only unsolved mystery in Rose Hill.

ARTHUR

Sorry, its none of my business. I should not have opened my mouth. But she does keep herself to herself.

CHARLES

Too young for me? Not, not really. I am too old for her. There is a difference.

ARTHUR

If you say so. We can talk about something else.

CHARLES

Pas de problème. No, that's fine; I have no secrets. (*pause*) Soon, Zoe will be too old for me.

ARTHUR

How can she become too old for you ?

CHARLES

When she is too old for me, she will leave. She will have outgrown me. An older man, a younger girl, it is a very ancient story, a very well known story, always with a bad ending. But it is interesting along the way. Certainly, Zoe, will leave me one day. She may even find herself an American boy. (*pause)*

What does that mean, what you said earlier? "All of my friends are one drink women".

ARTHUR

Whatever you want it to mean.

CHARLES

Philosophy and poetry in eight words. Chapeau, Sheriff. You've given me eight words to ponder on. They ponder often, don't they, in Westerns ?

ARTHUR

I guess so.

CHARLES

Those eight words might even constitute a lie that I can believe.

ARTHUR

Maybe. *(pause)* How are you adjusting to life in America?

CHARLES

I can't answer that Arthur.

ARTHUR

Really ? Why not? You've been here for a few years. No thoughts so far? No impressions? Either good or bad?

CHARLES

I meant that I'm not definite about actually living in America. Is Rose Hill typical? I don't think that it is.

ARTHUR

That is for sure. So how are you adjusting to Rose Hill then?

CHARLES

Assez bien, well enough.

ARTHUR

Once you feel that you've adjusted completely, it will be time to leave. If you wait too long, you won't be able to leave.

CHARLES

I will remember that. You make remaining here sound ominous. Are you speaking from experience?

ARTHUR

Well... (*cut off by Charles*)

CHARLES

She's dancing now. Irma is quite versatile   (*indicates Irma offstage with his chin*)

IRMA

(*offstage*) Does anyone recognize this dance? I am not very good at dancing, it takes a carefree attitude that I was never able to master. It requires someone light on their feet, that isn't me. But today, I'm doing ok, apparently. My partner calls himself Frank. He must be very skilled as a dancer, if I am able to follow his lead. He's whispering " I miss our dips together". He is quite the..oooohhh..... Frank says that you would remember this dance from......

CHARLES

The audience waits for a personal sign from the over there.

ARTHUR
(*laughs*) The over there. I see that you've acquired some Rose Hill jargon.

CHARLES
It's inescapable, like one of those countless, ugly billboards along the motor routes. I'm adding mystic to my list of languages half spoken.

ARTHUR
You could purchase one of those psychic/English dictionaires that they sell in the gift shop. In another six months, you would be fluent. (*pause*) So there are signs that the audience craves....
CHARLES
That they demand. If not their own individual situation, then for another member of the crowd. A random assembly such as this feels a unique kinship while it is together; it has a sense of unity. Human behavior can be so interesting. It's like a raffle where someone must win for the crowd to be satisfied.

ARTHUR
I used to organize scavenger hunts at family reunions. Each team would rather lose than be part of a game ending in a tie. I see the similarity.

CHARLES
Attends, Irma has finished and Madame Crystal is about to start her portion.

ARTHUR
I like the way that Cris walks among them, like a savior or a leper, and then, depending on what she says, they recoil in shame, or nearly faint from awe.

CHARLES
This is all so bizarre. Some of them need to tell their nearest friend or even a total stranger, it does not matter which, how correct Madame Crystal is, how precise she is with her comments.

ARTHUR

I sympathize with those who curse her as a fraud; everyone one has skeletons.

CHARLES

Apparently that includes the skeletons themselves. The crowd accepts all of this as an affirmation of her gift. It reminds me of a Las Vegas nightshow.

ARTHUR

You've been to Las Vegas?

CHARLES

For the French tourist, it is mandatory to see Las Vegas (*pause*). Las Vegas est incontournable.
(*Irma arrives in a rush*)

CHARLES/ARTHUR

Hi Irma/Good morning.

IRMA

Hi guys. I can only stay for a minute, I'm booked most of the day with appointments.

CHARLES

Crystal just told one of them to stop drinking. His problem with alcohol is obvious to a blind man.

IRMA

Yeah, but she has the guts to say it. That's take courage.

CHARLES

And that young girl, the one with the tattoo, Crystal is advising her to leave her boyfriend; he will only hurt you, she said.

ARTHUR

His name is Harold, apparently. He's too young for such an old name.

Look, he's embarrassed, ashamed. What a jerk. His denials are his confession. I've seen that often enough. Criminals try so hard at times; he is acting the same way.

IRMA

She's very effective, isn't she? Let's see how Harold's denial works.

CHARLES

He has decided to bluff it out. Defiance might work for him. Qui sait? Oh, Crystal has moved on another person.

IRMA

For once, she has left someone off the hook.

ARTHUR

Like you and Willie.

IRMA

Willie?

ARTHUR

Your spirit fisherman with the sombrero. You just spoke to him.

IRMA

Oh him. He was forgettable; the sombrero did not change his basic character. He was and is a forgettable man. I'm a chameleon, an interpreter to the other side. I don't stay one color for very long. Many of the spirits are unremarkable, the boring are no less boring when they are dead.

CHARLES

And the child, Meghan?

IRMA

Unforgettable, unfortunately. This job does have its drawbacks, like any other, I'd imagine. Well guys, I have other business to attend. A regular, special client has an appointment with me in 15 minutes. His wife may be late, but I must be on time. Arthur, will you be your office tomorrow or the next day, say around noon?

ARTHUR

Let's make it 3 o'clock.   A client who is both regular and special at the same time?

IRMA

Yes, I have two relationships that are both regular and special. That's one too many.   Ok, 3 pm, the day after tomorrow. That works. Bye. (*exits*).

CHARLES

Do you notice that Crystal only only gives advice to the tourists that she is physically able to touch?   Her gift is weak, I think.   There seems to be a range limitation to her ability, as if she is nearsighted. I had not noticed that before. Or perhaps her touching them is a ploy to make the tourist feel more involved.   I'm not certain where Crystal really stands.

ARTHUR

She's genuine. As a psychic, that is.

CHARLES

Yes. Crystal is clever.

ARTHUR

Cleverness can be a fatal flaw in a woman.

CHARLES

In anyone. This is the 1990s, everyone is equal. Sexism is passe. C'est ce qu'on dit. I read it in the local paper.

ARTHUR

So they say.   Equal but not the same (*pause*).   I am sick of change.(*pause*) Take that girl with the tattoo. I'd like to tell her, seriously my dear, tattooing is cattle branding by another name. I just don't understand this behavior, Charles. It is self destructive, demeaning. Is it self esteeming to disfigure yourself? If someone did this to her, I'd be asked to arrest him; if she does it to herself, its called art. Go figure, or go disfigure. When did this fad start?

CHARLES

Tattoos? 300 years ago? Its only a butterfly, Arthur.

ARTHUR

You're no help. (*pause*)

CHARLES

We're missing Crystal's show.

ARTHUR

You may be on to something, Charles, with Cris' method. Do you think that could be the sole difference between psychics and mediums, with the correct set of supernatural bifocals one could be both? But where to find such an optometrist?

CHARLES

You know very well this second sight jargon. (*pause*) Crystal is excellent at what she does.

ARTHUR

At what she does? (*winks*)

CHARLES

She fires up the crowd.

ARTHUR

She can certainly fire up some of the men in the village.
Including you Charles?

CHARLES

I'm already taken by the too young Zoe.

ARTHUR

Where is your wife, er, your girlfriend? I thought that she would enjoy the show, as there isn't much other entertainment in town.

CHARLES

Zoe doesn't like crowds.

ARTHUR

I don't see much of her, sometimes just a glimpse when she goes for her strolls, that's balade in French, I think.

CHARLES

Yes, balader.

ARTHUR

I'm surprised that I don't see you hiking with her more often. You spend more time with my son Buck than Zoe. (*silence, and Arthur changes subject*) Tourists are still arriving, the nearer parking lots must be filled by now. It's going to be a good day for business.

CHARLES

Crystal is really skilled at this, it's a pity that she is not the star event. She's attractive enough.

ARTHUR

She is that. Enough for any man, maybe even enough for two.

CHARLES

Un ménage à trois. You shock me Sheriff Arthur. Surely that is illegal in the US.

ARTHUR

Laws are different in the countryside.

CHARLES

I don't believe that. Tu plaisantes.

ARTHUR

Yes, I am. But they are definitely not the same in Rose Hill as they are elsewhere; it's a world onto itself.

CHARLES

(*Charles changing subject*) Buck and I like to watch the eagles and hawks. Predators are more interesting.

ARTHUR

What?

CHARLES

This is why Zoe and I rarely hike together. She enjoys stopping to listen to birdsong. I find it childish, and annoying.

ARTHUR

Zoe is little more than a child herself, er I mean that she seems very innocent.

CHARLES

Listening to birdsong, only stupid birds sing. She even has recordings of birdsong in the house. It's becoming an obsession with her.

BUCK

(*Buck enters*) Hey Chuck, Hi Dad. I see that Madame Crystal is just about done with her performance. She's only been here a few months, but she has really improved these public readings. It is less gloom and doom with her than it was before, with, what was her name?

ARTHUR

Cassie

BUCK

Yeah Cassie. What ever happened to her? (*Arthur and Charles shrug*) Well, Madame Crystal is much better. She can really whip up a crowd.

CHARLES

Your father was just saying the same thing, Buck.

BUCK

She is incredible. Boy, the thoughts and auras that she must receive but can't disclose.

CHARLES

It is required to be a family friendly show, I think.

ARTHUR

Supposed to be, yes.

BUCK

Her technique of near touches, and soft touches is like something from..

ARTHUR

It is reminiscent of a strip club

BUCK

I was going to say a revival meeting, Dad.

ARTHUR

Attendance at one can follow the other, I suppose. You can't have redemption without sin.

BUCK

You still see them around. Revivals, that is. Rose Hill draws them as a decoy draws geese. We are the wicked blot in God's country.

(*MC done with show, enters stage right*)

MC

Wicked? Is that new slang, Buck? A commentary on my reading? I like it.

BUCK

No, not at all, Madame Crystal. I was telling Dad and Chuck that what you and the other psychics do is misunderstood in some of the neighboring towns. They see us as the center of wickedness.

ARTHUR

That's old news, Buck. They call us heathens. We see them as rednecks and rubes. Again, old news. As always, Cris that was quite the performance.

MC

So wicked must mean wonderful. I can be very wicked, men. (*touches Arthur*) You know very well that it's not a performance Arthur, I save those for the less public venues (*winks at Charles*). What I do is closer to a scientific demonstration and it is not a circus act.

ARTHUR

Yes, ma'am. I stand corrected. You do it with such flair that your "science" approaches art.

CHARLES

Oui. Très artistique, Crystal.

MC

Artistic? You are saying that I am artistic? (*all men nod*). The compliment sounds more true in French, Charles. We should study together.

CHARLES

Lessons? What sort of lesson?

MC

Why, in French, of course. We could practice during your hikes; I could join you. You pass so many hours on them anyway. I'd be good company. I have strong legs, they are used to workouts.

CHARLES

Oh. I'm not...

MC

Did you think that I meant lessons in how I do my "psychic performances"?

BUCK

That's not a bad idea, Chuck. When I'm busy with the sawmill, you'd have another person along, in case...

ARTHUR

In case of what?

BUCK

Well, in case of an accident or a medical... it is not smart to hike alone at your age.. I mean at any age. I'm just saying..

MC

(*looking at Buck*) Or when Buck is busy at other times....I'm sure he has a social life... a girlfriend...

ARTHUR

What about Zoe, Cris? She is French as well, maybe you could learn with her. In exchange, you could teach her to be a psychic.

MC

That isn't possible. One either is or is not psychic. It is a talent, a gift, not a learned skill.

CHARLES

Not like French, apparently. Crystal is right, you have a business to run. We can still hike, but tomorrow with be French with my wicked student. A demain, Crystal.

MC

A Demain?

CHARLES

Until tomorrow. We will have our first lesson tomorrow. (*exits*)

MC

I must leave as well. These public reading fatigue me. Sometimes I feel that parts of me are being ripped out, snatched from me by psychic groupies, and replaced by their thoughts, their emotions, their memories.

BUCK

The readings have that level of impact on you, Madame Crystal?

MC

Absolutely, Buck. I need time to ….to… to recover from this assault. To rebecome me.

ARTHUR

I had no idea Cris. I assumed that these readings were fun for you.

MC

In America, you become your job.

ARTHUR

That means that you are doing it well.

MC

You believe that? Anyone else would complain that it means that you have no life. My service here is valuable, but it is work. I really must go, now that the next medium, Ruth, is about to start her session. (*pause*) I hate the dead, they have nothing of value to contribute to the living.

BUCK

But they are the reason, or at least one of the reasons, that Rose Hill exists. Aren't they?

ARTHUR

The sine qua non…

BUCK

Is that French?

ARTHUR

Latin. The dead are essential to Rose Hill. La raison d'être.

BUCK

Latin?

ARTHUR

French.

BUCK

Can we stick with English, Dad?

MC

I disagree with both of you. The dead are the marquée, but not the real value.

ARTHUR

Sizzle, but not steak?

MC

Yes, they are nothing more than pacifiers.

ARTHUR

How is that, Cris?

MC

Another time, Arthur, when I'm less tired. I really must rest. (*exits*)

(*Drum roll offstage*)

ARTHUR

Stay for a minute Buck, we need to talk.

ACT 1

SCENE 2

(*Home of Zoe and Charles*)

CHARLES

J'en ai marre de ces américaines qui pensent savoir parler français. Celle-là me faisait penser à …

ZOE

..À une vache espagnole (*Zoe finishes Charles' sentence, laughing*)

CHARLES

Non, ma petite clairvoyante. Tu as tort. J'allais dire Buck.

ZOE

Buck, ton bon ami?

CHARLES

L'ami de quelqu'un bien sûr. Tu as quand même, à moitié raison. Pas une vache espagnole, mais plutôt un bœuf américain. Il est fort, ce Buck.

ZOE

Tu le trouve ainsi; je ne l'ai pas remarque.

CHARLES

Vache, bœuf, la vraie blague, comme tu viens de le dire, c'était cette (*knock at door, Charles answers and Madame Crystal steps right in*)

MC

Bonjour Charles. I thought that we could start right away. We can begin now, I'm free most of the morning. Oh!, Hi, Zoe. Bonjour. (*attempts to shake hands, but Zoe avoids contact*)

CHARLES

Bonjour Crystal.

MC

This house is so cute, I see that you bring your enthusiasm for birds inside.

ZOE

(*cold*) Begin what, Madame Crystal?

MC

Lessons, Zoe. French lessons. These photos are exquisite; you took them yourself, Charles? You are so talented.

Yesterday we were all talking after the public readings, you should have been there, it's like a French market day.

ZOE

I'm sure that it isn't.

MC

Anyway, Charles offered to give me French lessons.

CHARLES

(*smiling*) You offered, and I agreed.

ZOE

She offered what?

MC

Well, I did offer to do a group reading for you two; here take my hand (*reaches to Zoe, who recoils quickly*)

CHARLES

You did? I don't recall. We don't really take to that. We stay away from this psychic (*pause*) stuff.

MC

Of course you do, you must take to it. Everybody enjoys being read, especially those who say that they don't. You can't live in the heart of Rose Hill and not take to psychics. Can a Frenchman not like wine?

CHARLES

I am half Swiss, neutrality is in my blood.

MC

I could even do a short reading here, right now (*reaches again toward Zoe, who once again withdraws and turns to make coffee, now with back to MC and Charles*)

ZOE

Perhaps another time, Madame Crystal. If you are going to study French, I don't understand why you think that you should take private lessons. Surely you don't need them.

CHARLES

Why not? It might be fun, refreshing. It would be different at least. (*scanning MC from head to toe, but MC does not see this appraisal*)

ZOE

(*turns to face MC and Charles*) Who would you even converse with, other than Charles? This is not a French speaking region. In fact, I not even sure that this is an English speaking region.

MC

We could have conversations, Charles and me primarily, but of course with you as well.

ZOE

Me? You and I have absolutely nothing in common; we are years apart in age, and so different from each other. Don't Americans, even Hungarian Americans say that three is a crowd?

MC

Our age difference is less than the gap between you and Charles.

ZOE

We do more together than speak to each other in French, much more.

MC

And we are not really that different from each other. Undoubtedly, a reading would confirm that.

ZOE

No. I have better things to do than readings, or to listen to unnecessary French lessons. Enjoy yourselves; I'm going for a walk.

CHARLES

No, stay. We'll leave. I'm not sure how long this first lesson will last. Crystal, give me a few minutes and I will meet up with you at the lake gazebo. Un rendez-vous.

MC

A rendez-vous, oh, that's French isn't it? Wonderful. It might be simpler for us to just swing by my place instead. I'll wait for you outside.

CHARLES

D'accord. OK.

MC

Perfect. Bye Zoe. (*exits*)

ZOE

(*angrily*) Quel cochon tu es. Tu cours sans cesse après les jupes des filles. J'en ai marre de ces américaines qui veulent savoir parler français.

CHARLES

It is only lessons.

ZOE

And you should have learned your lesson by now.

CHARLES

I'm worried about the sheriff.

ZOE

Why, is he a competitor of yours? Does he have more notches on his pistol than you do?

CHARLES

I am talking about our business.

ZOE

Our business? Then why do you involve yourself with this Madame Crystal? If I had known three years ago…

CHARLES

I must disarm the sheriff.

ZOE

He does not even carry a weapon.

CHARLES

Yes, he does. He is clever, he carries his weapon concealed. That is his nature. He conceals. He conceals his pistol, his ability, everything he conceals. I am the eagle and he is the fox. It is difficult, but not impossible for the fox to conceal himself from the eagle.

ZOE

You overestimate Arthur.

CHARLES

I must be better at this game than he.

ZOE

If you are so confident that Arthur is as skilled as you say that he is, then you overestimate yourself. A game, you say? Is is still a game if Arthur is not participating? It is certainly not petanque that occupies us here. No, I'm wrong, tout a fait tort. Bon, alors, let's call it a game. You've won enough at this roulette table. It is time to collect our winnings and leave.

CHARLES

I must be better at it than he is, if we wish to remain here in Rose Hill. And Arthur cannot not play. It is what he does. He may not play it as well as he did 20, 30 years ago as a young man. Perhaps neither do I. (*pause*) He has even spoken of retirement.

ZOE

Tant mieux. You can both retire together. You call youself an eagle and Arthur a fox, but I see you as the fox, and the sheriff as a hound. You could retire together and find a new, what is the word, not a career, but a, passe-temps, yes, a hobby together. Maybe painting. Something for two old men. (*pause, goes to take his hand*) I did not mean to say old.

CHARLES

It is more true than not. (*pause*) His retirement would be a catastrophe for us. A tired hound is ideal when one is an old fox, tired of running.

ZOE

Do we?

CHARLES

Do we need Arthur to remain as the sheriff?

ZOE

No. Do we need to remain in Rose Hill? We could run our business anywhere; after two years, we have assimilated enough, and earned enough. I miss Paris. We could move to New York, or even Los Angeles. Birds are everywhere.

CHARLES

Rose Hill is perfect for our business. It is an easy place in which to live.

ZOE

It is an easy place for the dead to reside, but they do so only temporarily. But for the living?

CHARLES

Probably not.

ZOE

Definitely not. It is a constant struggle for the truly alive to live in this cemetery. And that is what the alive are supposed to do, to live. Life is so painful for me here.

CHARLES

Je sais bien que tu es triste.

ZOE

Everyone is so fixated on the dead here; I look in the mirror and I see shadows. Do you remember the mirrors at Versailles? The foreign tourists rave about them. But they are full of imperfections and wear. They are covered in black stains. After centuries, those mirrors are exhausted.

CHARLES

You are as beautiful as the day that I met you Zoe. I'll replace the mirror.

ZOE

Tu ne me comprends pas. I am the mirror. Let's flee from this cemetery while we still live. While I am still young, while we are still young. This family of foxes can start over elsewere. If you insist, we can visit here again when we are dead.

CHARLES

Later, Zoe. The money is very good here and neither of us actually work.

ZOE

Speak for yourself. You repeat that phrase over and over. You say time and again that what we do is not work, knowing that it is not true. I am working myself into grave after grave. Soon, one of them will be my own.

CHARLES

We will discucc this again later, after the lesson

ZOE

She is dangerous, this Crystal.

CHARLES

I'm attracted to that sort, you must recognize that by now, Zoe. You are the most dangerous of all.

ZOE

I thought that you loved me, Charles.

CHARLES

I do.

ZOE

Yet you call me dangerous.

CHARLES

You know that I mean dangerous as a compliment.

ZOE

I am just an ordinary woman Charles.

CHARLES

A woman of course, but certainly not ordinary.

(*exits and Zoe walks and starts birdsong record*)

ZOE

You overestimate the sheriff, you overestimate yourself, and yet you underestimate me. (*knock at door a minute, Zoe goes slowly to answer it*) Come in Buck, Charles is not here.

BUCK

I know, I saw Chuck and Madame Crystal walking toward her house. They must be starting lessons.

ZOE

You could say lessons, yes. Wait, you know about this?

BUCK

Sure, it came up at the town square yesterday. Between the spirit talk, and the Latin and French, it was difficult for me to follow the conversation. But yeah, Madame Crystal decided to have French lessons. I'm not sure why, but she thought it was a good idea. I encouraged Chuck to go along.

ZOE

You did ? Why?

BUCK

Its obvious, Zoe.

ZOE

(*kisses Buck*) You have the best of bad intentions Buck.

BUCK

Did I do wrong?

ZOE

No, you did well. But this Madame Crystal is such a spiteful woman. I don't know where to begin describing her faults.

BUCK

Really, she's always been nice to me. Dad went off on her to me yesterday. He said some things about her past that perhaps he shouldn't have.

This town can make me tense. It used to be different. People are so complex, so angry and bitter. Trees are kinder, most of them at least.

ZOE

You don't find that most people are also kind? The native born Americans have welcomed us warmly. Charles and your Dad, they are friends.

                    BUCK
That is because they are both immigrants. Even we natives find ourselves as immigrants at a certain point, at a certain age. Or so says my father, who has apparently reached that age.

                    ZOE
I don't understand what your father means by that?

                    BUCK
I don't either. It must be an age thing.

                    ZOE
Buck, Blanche Neige.

                    BUCK
What is that?

                    ZOE
Snow White.

                    BUCK
I don't understand.

                    ZOE
It isn't important.   I should have said mon chevalier blanc, my white knight.

                    BUCK
I like that one much better.   Oh, I signed another lumber contract today. They say that money does not grow on trees, but it does for me. Some folks, even some of my customers, ridicule me because I am a tree whisperer.

                    ZOE
I've never heard a bad word said about you, Cheri. Is it a good contract?

BUCK

Yes, very. It's going to be another profitable season. We might be able to act sooner than we thought.

ZOE

Wonderful ! This is wonderful. Let's act now, before it is too late.

BUCK

In a year, two at the most...

ZOE

A year?

BUCK

Or two. Sales are going nowhere but up. Even Chuck may consider me crazy, but I know which trees to harvest. The ones that I select are among the best, and my clients recognize it. Death is a part of life, here in Rose Hill, death is life, or at least it offers a living to me, and it will for us.

Even the eagles that so intrigue Chuck. They prefer a dead, or dying, tree in which to construct their nest.

Dad told Madame Crystal that there is an art to her psychic science. I feel the same way about mine.

ZOE

What did she reply to that?

BUCK

I don't remember, that's when they started talking about French lessons.

ZOE

I see. This new contract will help us immensely. You've done fantastic work, Buck, bt there is more to do. We need to escape this horrid village and abandon death to the dead. Soon.

BUCK

Death? Why are you so fearful, my love? You're shaking (*holds her*) This town is safe, my Dad has a perfect record. You are safe here with him, with me. There is no death here. I'm talking about felling trees, Zoe, not real death. I leave that to people like Irma and Ruth, and the other mediums. (*pause*)

ZOE

Je sais. I know. But soon? We can act soon? I'm anxious.

BUCK

Sure Zoe, soon. Hey, I learned a French phrase today.

ZOE

Oh?

BUCK

Que tu es beau (*kisses Zoe*).

ZOE

(*laughing*) It's belle, not beau, Buck.

BUCK

I ruined it, didn't I?

ZOE

No, not if you say it again, correcty. I like the sound of it.

BUCK

Que tu es belle. (*another kiss*)

Lets go for a hike together, we can listen to live birdsong instead of this recording (*stops birdsong*) . You can sing to me.

ZOE

I will sing. But you must promise me to sing in return. Birds can sing, why shouldn't we?

ACT 1

SCENE 3

(*home of Madame Crystal, late morning*)

CHARLES

Bon. Crystal, cela nous suffira aujourd'hui. That's enough class for today. You are a very apt student.

MC

Someone told me once that in learning a foreign language as an adult, one learns best on a pillow.

CHARLES

On a pillow?

MC

In bed.

CHARLES

That's a bit forward.

MC

I'm receptive.

CHARLES

Receptive to what?

MC

Many things. And you? Are you open?

CHARLES

Open to what?

MC

Oh, many things. Are you open to a reading, for instance?

CHARLES

A reading? Poof. Why? I have no worries, no unanswered questions.

MC

I can tell from our closeness, even from our short time together today that you are a strong man. I'd like to know more. You're dark.

CHARLES

You must say that to all of your male clients.

MC

Only the strong ones.

CHARLES

But I am not a client, and I don't wish to be one.

MC

You could be much more than a client to me.

CHARLES

(*walking around room*) And this dark strength of mine attracts you; you cannot resist it. Instead of being repelled by it, you are drawn. I don't know how to respond.

MC

You make it sound like a cheap romance novel.

CHARLES

Should I unbutton my shirt? Isn't that the first step in such novels? I'm only going by what I've seen on the book covers. So?

MC

If you're warm. It is July. You don't repel me, but drawn to you? (*pause*) It's too early to say whether I am attracted or only curious. (*pause*) I simply find you interesting, and yes, somewhat mysterious.

CHARLES

I am not psychic, but I know people.

MC

Women, you mean?

CHARLES

Only women know women. I know people. I understand desire (*picks up a travel book on France*). Hmmm. "Traveling in France". Have you been to France, Crystal?

MC

I visited France many years ago; I'd like to return there some day, it would be more enjoyable if I were to have the right companion.

CHARLES

Someone who speaks the language?

MC

Ça va de soi. Is that right?

CHARLES

Yes, very good. You learn quickly.

MC

I'd better not learn too quickly. I don't want to not need a companion.

CHARLES

In that case, you would need a guide and not this mysterious companion. He'd be stong and dark as well, I suppose?

MC

Oh, a guide would not be adequate. A companion would offer a deeper experience.

CHARLES

We'll see. (*pause*) One of these mediums should write a travel guide, like Fodors or Steve Reeves.

MC

That's a fantastic idea.   It would be a Michelin guide for the hereafter.

CHARLES

Intriguing, but who would write this?

MC

Very simple, a ghostwriter.

CHARLES

I hope that the afterlife is pun free. One of the mediums told me that spirits cannot lie in the over there, that they are only able to speak the truth.

MC

Which one? Which medium told you that?

CHARLES

As far as I know, there is only one…

MC

Only one medium? Charles, there are at least a dozen within 200 meters of us.

CHARLES

You don't know her.

MC

So, about your reading. If you would participate in one, then Zoe would surely sit with me to do hers.

CHARLES

No, that won't happen.

MC

There is nothing to fear.

CHARLES

There is always something to fear, Crystal.

MC

She fears the truth?

CHARLES

She fears your truth. We all do. We fear each other's truth. Each of us has our own truth, it is a fragile companion. It is not strong like your dark, mysterious companion. It doesn't react well went confronted with the truth of strangers.

MC

We are not strangers. Anyway, truth is truth...

CHARLES

You're wrong Crystal. There is no objective truth.

MC

Really?

CHARLES

Sure. (*laughs*) That is my truth.

MC

Touché. This has been a much deeper conversation than I was expecting. Let's switch to a subject less manly, something more elegant..

CHARLES

Is that code for simple?

MC

Tell me what you find most attractive about me.

CHARLES

That is definitely a subject less manly. Without question, it would be your shyness and modesty.

MC

Those are two qualities.

CHARLES

You are too special to have only one best quality.

MC

But those are the same quality, shyness and modesty. That's like being given a pair of earrings and being told that they are two gifts.

CHARLES

I don't understand. Shyness and modesty are the same? Perhaps I used the wrong word, I tried to express calin, caline for you.

MC

Clever?

CHARLES

Yes, clever like a fox. Shy like a fox.

MC

(*laughs*) Sly like a fox. .

CHARLES

Yes, that is it. I see that there is more than one grammar police in town. (*pause*) How did you know the word "calin"?

MC

(*serious*) It just popped into my head. I must be psychic. (*laughs*) Slyness and modesty, two gifts after all. (*kisses Charles on cheek*) So, you see me as clever? This does not frighten you?

CHARLES

Pas du tout. I am a strong man, as you just told me yourself.

MC

According to you, my other most attractive quality is my modesty. You don't really think me modest, do you Charles?

CHARLES

Je te l'explique. It is your lack of modesty that attracts me. You see what you want and you immediately target it, or him. You don't possess the eyes of a doe, of a prey, but those of a bird of prey.

MC

How on Earth did you ever attach yourself to Zoe? Her name even rhimes with Doe.(*pause*)   Oh, I understand now. Its so obvious.   She attached herself to you.

CHARLES

It was mutual. It reads as a very long story, Crystal. I don't have the time and I don't have the desire to recount it today.

MC

What do you desire today? (*no response*) Hmm, a long story, and yet you and she have only been together for what, three years?

CHARLES

I've known you less time, Crystal. What is our story? Long or short?

MC

Short, but getting longer, I hope.

CHARLES

Hmm.   When I was learning English, whatever I told my teacher seemed to be confidential.

MC

Confidential in what way?

CHARLES

It was as if saying something in English was safe, as if I hadn't said anything at all, since it was spoken in a foreign language.

MC

Interesting.   It would be like writing on a chalkboard and then immediately erasing it.

CHARLES

We had a secret language, I could be more open, as we seemed to have a private language between the two of us. Of course, it wasn't true, but I enjoyed it.

MC

And your teacher, did he,

CHARLES

She..

MC

I should have known. And your teacher, did she view this in the same manner as you?

CHARLES

I don't know. It could be. She pretended well. It didn't concern me one way or the other.

MC

Is that another of your own truths?

CHARLES

Yes. Yes it is. Tout à fait correct, Crystal.

MC

I can pretend. (*pause*) We can make our story elegante. Simple and complicated.

And private, like our own language. At the moment, it is complicated, but there are methods to simplify it.

CHARLES

We are both beginning to speak in riddles.

MC

It's a dance. Do you recall the public reading from yesterday?

                              CHARLES
        I remember the part about the dance with dips.

                                MC
        Exactly, we are dancing.

ACT I

SCENE 4

(home of Madame Crystal, around 1 PM, knock at door, MC answers, Arthur enters)

ARTHUR

Hi Cris *(kiss)*, How is my favorite psychic? *(kiss)*. Still sweet, I see. Sweet as cherry pie.

MC

Cherry pie is only for dessert. On the other hand, if you ask me out to dinner again, I wouldn't say no.

ARTHUR

You can be very forward. I like that.

MC

I've been told that before, recently. Someone has to lead.

ARTHUR

That is the man's role.

MC

If the man is strong. Are you strong, Sheriff?

ARTHUR

You've told me before that I am. Nothing has changed as far as I can determine. Thank goodness. So this is my role?

MC

Only if you play it. I know that you aren't shy. Like me. Yes, you are still strong, but you are not like your son.

ARTHUR

Thank goodness for that as well. How are we different?

MC

I've been in Pennsylvania long enough to at least know the names of trees.

ARTHUR

I'm overjoyed to hear it. You may know more about the forest flora than I do. A tree is a tree is a tree. I was never much interested in trees.

MC

Unlike your son.

ARTHUR

Well it doesn't take a psychic to see that.

MC

That is a very old line, it was funny once. In a previous life (*both laugh*) (*pause*) Buck is like a board of white pine, blank and soft. Pine is very good for some purposes, but useless for others.

ARTHUR

And the father?

MC

Oh, he is strong, he is red oak, or cherry.

ARTHUR

You taste like cherry. Maybe we are of the same species, we make a good pair.

MC

But you have a dark side.

ARTHUR

Don't we all?

MC

All men?

ARTHUR

I meant all people. Or in our case, all us cherry trees.

MC

I'm trying to be serious, Arthur. We all behave as if the rules don't apply to us. You yourself complain about some laws; you who are paid to enforce them. You expect compliance with social norms, and then you proceed to ignore them yourself.

ARTHUR

So what, I have a dark side. Do you want to read me, as you say, to find it?

MC

No. (*Arthur surprised*). I turn myself off around you.

ARTHUR

I'm disappointed. I was trying to turn you on as they used to say.

MC

My powers, I turn them off.

ARTHUR

Your powers (*laughs*)

MC

(*slaps arm*) My sensitivity, then. I've learned about you through it. It would not be as amusing if I knew everything about you. Cheating is not always fun.

ARTHUR

You would be the first, Cris, a woman that prefers to not know all of a man's secrets.

MC

I know too many of them as it is.

ARTHUR
I only have a few secrets; I wouldn't say that I have many.

MC
Men invariably tell anyone who will listen that they have few secrets. It is never true.

ARTHUR
Never?

MC
Your son, the white pine, is the exception that proves the rule. But even he has one or two.

ARTHUR
Let ;s talk about me, not my son. You just told me that you disengage your psychic abilities aound me.

MC
I do. I know too many secrets of too many others. They start to become repetitive.

A day in Rose Hill can be like watching the same sitcom over and over. Only the commercials are different. Sooner or later, you will realize how stupid it all is.

ARTHUR
I'm behaving badly, that's rude. How are you doing, Cris? You seem to be depressed today, definitely more serious than usual. Yesterday, before leaving the square, you were exhausted.

MC
It must have been a combination of the crowd size and the heat. The gazebo is too small for public readings, but we need some kind of coverage is case of rain or heat.

I'm back to normal.

ARTHUR
Is being back to normal good or bad? Or is it wicked?

MC

Good, I think, very good and wicked.

ARTHUR

That is more like it. I enjoy wicked, with chocolate. I do have a serious question of my own to ask you. Why do you hate the dead? You nearly screamed it yesterday, right before you left to recuperate. They are beyond doing anyone harm.

MC

I'll answer this, but only briefly, I could go on for hours, but that would only raise my blood pressure and bore you. When it comes to blood pressure, I prefer that we raise each other's together.

So, these spirits that "report back", they must have been the most unobservant people when alive. The only advice that they proffer to their living relatives is "don't worry, be happy". Is the afterlife really that carefree?

Do they ever provide any details on "living" conditions over there, not even any jokes or interesting spirtis that they have met. It mustn't be very exciting

ARTHUR

It may be too amazing for words.

MC

Surely the dead have other things to do than comfort the living. That is all that they can do in any case for the living. No, I am convinced that the dead, especially dead men, having nothing to contribute to humanity. A great percentage of the living don't offer much either.

ARTHUR

Especially the men?

MC

Yes.

ARTHUR

So you hate men?

MC

You know that I don't. No, I like men very much. They are a weakness, like chocolate.   I hate their toys and the foolish way that men play with them.

ARTHUR

Toys? Like motorcycles?

MC

Fantasies is a better word. Men have created three fantasies.

ARTHUR

Only three? I enjoy more than three fantasies by myself per day. Before lunch.

MC

Three useless but dangerous fantasies.

ARTHUR

Let me guess. Is the first one this village?

MC

Wrong. You are so far afield; in fact this village counteracts fantasy, it is an antidote to fantasy.

ARTHUR

I've never heard Rose Hill described in quite that way. Well, I give up already, what are these three fantasies?

MC

Sports, politics, and religion. None of these so called achievements accomplish anything, other than to waste time and breath. Men participate and argue about these three mirages as if they had any significance. They are the true phantoms.

Worse, men have no real control over them.   It's hilarious and nauseating at the same time. Men waste a great portion of their lives with these objects, behaving as boys do with toy soldiers and castles of sand.

I've come to accept it, like a balding man. He has no ability to reverse his receding hairline while I have little success in convincing him to stop worrying about it. The most I can do is the distract him.

ARTHUR
You distract well. What were we discussing, elevating our blood pressure?

MC
Arthur, you are not an exception to this disease, simply less afflicted than the majority of your kind.

ARTHUR
Tell me more, this is great for my self esteem. Speaking of secrets, I know yours, Cris.

MC
(*surprised, then smiles*) Oh, so you know my secret. We all need to have at least one. Perhaps we can combine one of yours and one of mine and create our own shared secret. I minored in drama, you know? (*Arthur shakes head no*). Now you do. (*Arthur and MC embrace*)

ACT I

SCENE 5

(*town square, the next morning*)

(*Irma and Crystal talking, calls to Zoe who approaches reluctantly*)

IRMA

I'm seeing Derk today.

MC

Your special client? The widower from Manhattan?

IRMA

That's the one.

MC

You shouldn't become more involved with him that you already are. It should remain a business relationship.

IRMA

I disagree. Our professional relationships begin as and are based on personal involvement, very personal. Our business is personal.

IRMA

Oh hi, Zoe. Come over and talk to us, I wont bite. And if Crystal does bite you, I'll run you over to the vet for a rabies vaccine.

ZOE

Hello Irma, Madame Crystal.

IRMA

I'm not sure that we've ever met like this before, in public.

ZOE

You two are so busy, and I've things to do.

MC

You do? Such as what?

ZOE

Normal things, I have a house and husband to care for.

IRMA

We are like three witches meeting at midnight.

MC

Except that it is the middle of the day, Irma.   Zoe, I didn't know that you and Charles had made it official. You are now married?

ZOE

Nearly. No, Irma, you and Madame Crystal are the witches. Don't include me in your special club. You two are always stirring trouble, if not with others, then between yourselves. You behave like indolent crows.

MC and IRMA

Caw, Caw. (*imitating crows*)

ZOE

Yes, crows. I prefer songbirds.

IRMA

I'm sorry, Zoe. It was a poor joke. But I see you so rarely that I don't even know how to speak with you. Sometimes a joke breaks the ice. It can be a good conversation starter. It backfired on me, sorry. So what type of birds do you like to listen to? Me, I enjoy hearing whip-poor-wills and cardinals.

ZOE

I like those ones too.

IRMA

Do you miss the songbirds of France?

ZOE

I have recordings of those, as well as American birds. I especially like the happy songs. They don't record the birds' distress calls.

MC

Men do that; they suppress and ignore the cries of the female, irregardless of the species.

IRMA

We're not birds, we can fly away. Unless we're injured. How are you Zoe?

ZOE

I am well. (*to MC*): I hear that you are effective in your readings, simply amazing. Congratulations.

MC

Did Buck tell you that? Would you like a private reading? I'm available immediately. Irma, Zoe and I will see you later, after....

ZOE

No, not really. I prefer a simple, private life. A reading would not tell me anything that I don't already know.

MC

You'd be surprised.

ZOE

I don't like to be surprised.

IRMA

Zoe, you are a surprise. Most girls....

ZOE

I just like to hear happy songs, beautiful songs.

MC

Sing us a song then. Sing us something pretty Zoe. Tell us your story.

ZOE

My story is my story, pretty or not.

IRMA

It looks very pretty to me.

ZOE

Do you think that your powers change you?

IRMA

Yes. There is no doubt of that.   A medium and her, or his, powers are one and the same. You are they and they are you.

MC

My powers haven't changed me.

IRMA

Crystal, either it is different for non-medium psychics..

MC

There you go again with mediums are the best…

IRMA

Or else you are not as observant as everyone knows you to be. Even Zoe is aware of your talents, and she hasn't ever attended a public reading.

MC

 Buck does. He told her.

IRMA

Who cares? If he did, what does it matter? It only goes to prove my point,that you are good at what you do.

MC

And thus, according to you, mediums are better than us regular psychics.

                              IRMA
I compliment you and you take it as an insult. Ok, lets continue down
that path.

                              ZOE
Which path ? I need to return home.

                              IRMA
No, please stay just a little longer. I'll answer your question after I've
answered Crystal's.
(*facing MC*) You do very well at readings, too well.

                              MC
How can I do too well?

                              IRMA
You can't help but show off, to be too precise, too much on point. It
isn't good for them.

                              ZOE
Them? The spirits?

                              MC
I don't talk with spirits.

                              IRMA
(*shakes head no*) No, not...

                            CRYSTAL
I lost any interest in the dead a very long time ago.

                              IRMA
So you've told me, many times.

                              ZOE
The tourists?

IRMA

Yes. Crystal goes too far with them.

MC

Did you ever think that you don't go far enough?

IRMA

Oh, I'll be going far enough, soon enough.

ZOE

Irma...

IRMA

You had a question about our powers. Do they change us? For me, yes.
I won't speak for Crystal, she evidently has her own opinion, however wrong it is. It changes you, like the broom of a cleaning lady

MC

(*sighs*) Really? Like the broom of a cleaning woman?

IRMA

Or the broom of a witch. (*Zoe smiles*) Oh good Zoe, you understood my joke.

Yes, that is how I think of it. A maid sweeps up the rubbish of other people's lives, but when she leaves, she carries away with her, in her nostrils, in her hair, on her clothes, the dust of other people's lives. She can wash it out, we can't.

ZOE

And if you can't bathe it off...

IRMA

You eventually become filthy, like an untouchable in India. The dirt can make you sick.

MC

That is complete nonsense. I do have my own opinion on our power. You treat it like a doctor does his work. If you scrub well enough, and leave the work at the office, life can be normal.

IRMA

Is life normal for you?

MC

Of course it is.

ZOE

The same as it was for you even a year ago?

MC

No, yes, maybe. Life changes.

IRMA

But people don't ?

ZOE

Are you the same?

MC

This is a stupid conversation. Its the sort of one that men would have.

IRMA and ZOE

One that men would have?

MC

Yes. Have you ever listened to conversations among men? They raise such important questions and new ideas. Who cares about the answers? I don't. They can be so silly at times.

IRMA

Here we are, the three most beautiful witches in Rose Hill and none of us are married.

ZOE

Beautiful and single, what could be better than this? But you keep including me in your covent. I am not a witch.

MC

From what I understand, you have bewitched a young man in town. And yet you are a kept woman.

ZOE

What is a kept woman?

MC

Tu es une femme entretenue.

ZOE

(*slaps MC and storms off*)

IRMA

Why did you say that to Zoe? She was right to slap you.

MC

That is why I said it.

IRMA

You wanted her to slap you. I dont understand why.

MC

I'm old enough to be experienced in insults. I was the recipient of my own unfair quota when I was married. But at the end, it was I who delivered the best insult. (*pause*) The young don't appreciate that words have power. (*laughs*) I wanted her to strike me. I didn't know what to say in order to make her angry enough to lash out. Now I do. Caw, Caw, Caw.

IRMA

Oh stop with the crow call.   Here comes Buck.

BUCK

What happened? I looked up to see Zoe running off.   Was she feeling sick?

MC

No she seemed fine. Irma was teasing her..

IRMA

No, I wasn't.

MC

And then I must have said something that was misintrepeted. She was really mad, she went so far as to slap me. (*Irma looking on in disbelief*). I tried something in French that Charles taught me, and it came across wrong.

BUCK

I've done that myself.

MC

It wasn't as if I deliberately tried to make her angry (*surprised look from Irma*)

IRMA

Well…

MC

Yes?

IRMA

Nothing. Buck, it's the same with the spirits, sometimes a conversation is going so well, and then it goes off track; either I didn't undertand something that they said, they can be vague at times, as if they lose interest.

MC

The other day you indicated that neighboring villages consider us as devils. They are not entirely wrong. We're not angels, neither we nor the clients who come here by the thousands.

There are rare exceptions, you are an exception, Buck. You read as a blank, as a white board.

BUCK

Like a board of white oak from my sawmill?

MC

I was going to say something softer, like pine, but yes like that. A board of white oak. Unless this is an act, a ruse? Are you a good actor, Buck?

BUCK

I don't think so. Sometimes during the holidays, we let the local schools have plays at the sawmill. I lock up all the machines of course. Those plays don't have roles for anyone my age.

MC

Zoe mentioned her Charles being her husband, actually she said that she was nearly married. Maybe they could have a reception at at the same place as those plays, it's big enough.

BUCK

Oh, she said that? I hadn't heard about any marriage.

IRMA

This was really my first occasion to speak with Zoe. She isn't what I expected. I thought that she was just a gorgeous honey pot.

BUCK

What is a honey pot?

IRMA

A pretty young girl looking for a sugar daddy, a rich older man.

                              BUCK
That's not very nice, Irma.

                              IRMA
You're right Buck, it isn't. I glad that it isn't true. I was wrong. All it took was a few minutes in speaking with Zoe to realized that she loves Charles.

                              BUCK
She does? That's not...that's good. That is normal, isn't it?

                              MC
Maybe. Or it may be that her statement about being nearly married was wishful thinking.

                              BUCK
Wishful thinking?

                              MC
She may be protecting what she has, or forcing a decision on someone.

                              IRMA
Men don't like to be forced.

                              BUCK
Who, Charles?

                              MC
It could be Charles, or someone other than Charles.

                              MC
At some point a lumberman needs to stop surveying and start chopping. Just like a writer needs to stop reading at some point and set ink to paper.

                              BUCK
What does that mean? Oh, I like that. You're telling me that I should stop spectacting and begin participating.

MC

Yes. That's correct Buck. But I think that you've started participating already. At least that is my feeling. And my feelings are usually accurate.

IRMA

Buck, are you still looking for a house in town?

BUCK

Yes, but maybe only to rent, for a year or so. I'm wondering if I should buy or not. I might be making a change within 18 months or so.

IRMA

Sure, but I heard that one may be coming on the market. You know that houses in Rose Hill are good investments. Even for a short period.

BUCK

I'll stop by later and you can fill me in on the details. But right now, I need to go.

IRMA

Any time, Buck. You know where I live. See you later.

MC

Bye Buck. Don't say hello to her for me.

BUCK

Who?

MC

Your girlfriend. Bye Buck.

BUCK

Yeah, bye. (*exits*)

MC

I have little doubt that your first suspicion, about Zoe and Charles' relationship was correct. The honey pot and the sugar daddy. It's just that her current supplier might be running low on sugar.

IRMA

And whose fault is that if he is?

MC

She may have no choice but to find an American substitute.

IRMA

You would know that better than I. Her current sugar daddy may be pouring his sweetner into more than one coffee cup.

MC

Can you picture Charles as a real daddy? He'd be gone faster than you could say boo.

IRMA

He is definitely not father material; few men really are. What is your involvement in all of this, Crystal? You're beyond having children, so it makes no difference.

MC

My involvement is only to make folks happy. That includes making me happy.

ACT II

SCENE 1

(Sheriff's office)

ARTHUR

Zoe is a gold digger, Buck.

BUCK

There is no gold in Pennsylvania Dad, only wood and hard work

ARTHUR

You know what I mean Buck. You don't have enough gold, money, to keep Zoe grounded; she is so flighty, I expect her to float away on a strong breeze.

BUCK

How can you reach that conclusion? You've hardly spoken to Zoe.

ARTHUR

Not true. I've spoken to her on numerous occasions; she just hasn't responded.

BUCK

See?

ARTHUR

Yes, see. Her lack of conversational skills is evidence that she is shallow and uninteresting.

BUCK

You manage ok in French, Dad, you could try her native language.

ARTHUR

Buck, I've tried. She is bilingually boring. Not stupid, but vacuous.

                         BUCK
Vacuous?

                        ARTHUR
Empty. It is as if she is dead inside, or worse, perpetually absent.
Buck, you have not noticed this about her?

                         BUCK
No, not at first. But recently....

                        ARTHUR
Recently?

                         BUCK
Since their arrival here Zoe has become more withdrawn, whereas
Chuck seems more vivacious. See, I know some big words too. It means
lively. I think that Zoe is bored here.

                        ARTHUR
She has become bored with you?

                         BUCK
No, Dad, not with me.   I'm not a total loser. She is bored with Rose
Hill and with Chuck.

                        ARTHUR
She has told you that?

                         BUCK
Yes......in…

                        ARTHUR
Yes? Or yes, but?

                         BUCK
Just yes.

ARTHUR
I hope that you are positive about this Buck.

BUCK
I am. Chuck is too oppressive. I sometimes think that he is a vampire draining her of spirit

ARTHUR
I have it on good authority that vampires don't exist.

BUCK
They are not married

ARTHUR
I don't like where you appear to be going with this, son. They may not be husband and wife, but there are degrees of availability. Have you spoken to Chuck directly?

BUCK
No, of course not. Why would I ?   Zoe is almost ready to be rid of Chuck

ARTHUR
I am not one for soap operas. In all seriousness, this romance between you and the French couple is like Dark Shadows meets Peyton Place. Zoe and Charles may not endure as a couple, and your shenanigans, that's right, your shenanigans are not invisible to me Buck, will be to blame.

BUCK
My actions must be invisible to Chuck, or he just may not care. He is arrogant enough to take Zoe for granted. She is totally dependent on him. Other than his treatment of Zoe, he's a nice enough guy

ARTHUR
I think that he and I are agreed on that, Zoe cannot survive without him.

BUCK

Or someone like him.

ARTHUR

You? Buck, you do not resemble Charles in any way. Zoe doesn't work, and aside from your hikes in the woods.... Oh yes I am aware of those as well Buck. And aside from those she does nothing. I'm not even sure if she can read and write. I will need to..

BUCK

It is none of your business, Dad

ARTHUR

She is with Charles, Buck

BUCK

They are not married....

ARTHUR

This is the 90s son, the 1990s in Rose Hill. You are the last one who should be demanding normal conventions as far as marriage. Look, I'm concerned. If you and Zoe continue with this, will you move to France?

BUCK

I don't know. I think that you are worried about losing Charles, he is the nearest thing that you have to a friend.

ARTHUR

Friends come and go. I worry about Zoe's mental state as well.

BUCK

(*Laughs*) I was waiting for that insult. So, according to your investigation, I should avoid young, attractive, unmarried women who enjoy outdoor activities, especially those who are quiet and polite.

ARTHUR

You see quiet and polite, I see cunning and slow, almost dim.

BUCK

She can't be both cunning and slow.

ARTHUR

She is too mysterious.

BUCK

Finally, we agree. Mysterious. That is the attraction Dad.

ARTHUR

Oh well, I have work to do. Just be careful Buck. (*Buck exits*)
(*Irma enters, she and Arthur kiss*)

ARTHUR

If I'd known that you were coming for a kiss, I'd have suggested an earlier time.

IRMA

It was just a kiss.

ARTHUR

Your kisses are never just a kiss.

IRMA

That's sweet. But I am here on business.

ARTHUR

Ok, sure. What's the business?

IRMA

Madame Crystal. You need to do something about her.

ARTHUR

What exactly is the problem? Business or personal?

IRMA

It is a bit of both.

ARTHUR

Have you spoken to the city council about this? They are in charge of the business dealings in ths town. As far as the personal, it is between you and Cris.

IRMA

I will discuss my concerns with the council, I'd still like your help with it however. You'll see why in a minute. As far as the personal, it's not between myself, and Cris as you call her. It is between you and Cris.

ARTHUR

Let's focus on the business problem. Are you saying that Cris, Madame Crystal is a fake?

IRMA

No, that is not the worry...

ARTHUR

Because if you are, this town is very tolerant of a lot of things, including psychics who are obvious fakes...

IRMA

I know that..

ARTHUR

but who are seen as authentic by their clients. Its in the eye and mind of..

IRMA

of the believer.   I know all of this, Arthur. Crystal is not a faker. Her problem is her intensity. Charlatans just make things up as they go. Some tell you want you want to hear, others tell you what they want you to hear.

ARTHUR

You behave the same way. Heck, just the other day, the way that you spoke to that young child spirit, Meghan, and her mother.

IRMA

I speak the truth.

ARTHUR

Even when it hurts.

IRMA

Especially when it hurts. I provide them with peak pain, so that they can start the slide toward forgetting the pain.

ARTHUR

(*aloud but to himself*) Sliding towards oblivion. (*short pause*) Oh, just thinking aloud. Whereas Cris....

IRMA

She doesn't know when to stop. She has no self control. Our clients need to be cared for via a process, it is a regimen, not one séance and you are done. They mustn't be given all the medicine at one fell swoop.

ARTHUR

I see. Doing so is bad for business, and it eliminates repeat clients? Is that the issue, lower fees due Cris' effectiveness?

IRMA

I admit that it can be bad for business, her business. We don't really have the same client base. But worse that than it is bad for the customer seeking answers. The answers aren't always simple. Let me explain it this way. Patients don't see a psychologist or psychiatrist for their first session, and leave telling themselves, oh, I'm all better now; that was simple.

ARTHUR

I supect that some, if not many do.

IRMA

But you know very well that most don't.

ARTHUR

I'm aware of such thing. You may be right, who knows? Its outside of my expertise. So what do you expect of me? This still sounds like a topic for the next council meeting.

IRMA

Of course it is and it will be on the agenda. But before that, I'd like you to do some digging into Madame Crystal's past.

ARTHUR

What of you and your covent ? (*grins*) Can't they dig faster and better than I can ?

IRMA

We may have missed something. Psychics can be hard to read.

ARTHUR

I should put that on a bumper sticker.

IRMA

Plus, we need official documentation if we..

ARTHUR

We?

IRMA

The rest of the covent (*smiles*). If we are to have the council ask, or even demand that Crystal leave, we need to have a very good reason. Even to remove her name from the roll of psychics would be difficult without evidence. We just agreed that even obvious fakers, obvious to us at least, are members in good standing on the roll.

ARTHUR

I have done some research already, There isn't any hard evidence against her. She is a widow, no convictions for any crime. She seemed to have gone into the psychic business after the death of her husband. That doesn't strike me as unusual. In fact, widowhood almost seems to be a requirement.

IRMA

This is good to hear, but it doesn't help us against Crystal. You're right about widows and psychics. Many women who become psychics had been married to repressive men. Once they are swept away, the women blossom. Does that shock you ?

ARTHUR

I'm immune to shocks.

IRMA

That is too bad, Arthur. (*pause*) A moment ago, you said no hard evidence. Does that imply there exists another sort of evidence?

ARTHUR

Only rumors, gossip. Nothing actionable for your city council.

IRMA

Spill it, Arthur.

ARTHUR

Only you and Buck are privy to this. I don't remember why I mentioned this to him, he must have been gushing over her performance the other day. He is so naïve at times.

IRMA

I'm waiting.

ARTHUR

She was never charged.

IRMA

With what?

ARTHUR

You promise not to spread this around, correct?

IRMA

Correct. Charged with what?

ARTHUR

Murder.

IRMA

Murder? That would be perfect. For the village, I mean. Who was murdered?

ARTHUR

No one was murdered.

IRMA

But you just said......

ARTHUR

Cris' husband had been sick for a long time. He was somewhat older than she was. He died. A short time later, there were rumors that he had been murdered. Poison was the most popular theory apparently, as neither the doctor nor the staff at the crematorium noticed any obvious signs of foul play. There were not bullet holes or stab wounds that would have screamed murder. By the time the gossip made its way to the local police it was too late to do an investigation.

IRMA

Why was it too late?

ARTHUR

Cris had moved away, and notice that I said crematorium. There was neither suspect nor victim in town. Police budgets don't usually have a large account for "travel and accommodations to interview grieving widow in

parts unknown". There was no large insurance policy. So it was a dead end.
So to speak.

IRMA

Would you be able to investigate?

ARTHUR

I could, but I won't. It's an unprovable case.

IRMA

How do you know that it ?

ARTHUR

Believe me, I can see that this is important to you, Irma. But there is
nothing that I can do as law enforcement officer. Let me tell you a true story
that might explain my inaction.

IRMA

Sure, convince me.

ARTHUR

The mediums in this town are always going on about the afterlife. I get
that, it is their job. For some it is calling. They go on about how wonderful
it is, bright, and breezy, a regular land of milk and honey, although that
seems to be a very boring diet, not good at all for diabetics.

That was not my experience. I've been dead before. It was just
oblivion.

IRMA

You've been dead before? Shot in the line of duty?

ARTHUR

No, nothing as dramatic as that.

IRMA

Death is always a drama for the person playing the lead.

ARTHUR
Good point. No, I was murdered in a hospital, years ago.

IRMA
You're in good shape, considering.

ARTHUR
Thanks.

IRMA
Tell me the story, Arthur.

ARTHUR
This happened years ago, when I was working for a large department in California. Police work can be stressing, this job as Rose Hill chief is paid vacation by comparison.
One day, I had chest pains. So I drove myself to the ER and (*pause*)

IRMA
And?

ARTHUR
It was interesting. Men of my age, at that time, one with medical insurance and complaining of chest pains, well, we went pretty much right to the front of the queue.

IRMA
Especially a policeman.

ARTHUR
We'd be trumped by women in labor, of course. Would you call that sexist?

IRMA
To be trumped by women? I'd call that logical.

ARTHUR
In my case, I wasn't in my police uniform. It was a matter of their triage protocol. In their analysis, life threatening symptom and ability to pay the hospital bill ranks highly. So, Irma, they ran some tests and decided to admit me overnight.

Later that night, I have no idea exactly when, during the witching hour no doubt...

IRMA
That's when all sorts of eery things happen..

ARTHUR
This orderly, or medicine transporter, some person who has a plausible reason to be there at that time, came into my room. It was a semi private room. She rubbed this lotion on my chest and that was it. No pain, just darkness, nothingness. It was the closest to oblivion that I'd ever been to, up to that point, and even up to today.

IRMA
Wow! So what was it like for you on the other side? What did you see, hear, feel over there?

ARTHUR
It was oblivion, Irma. No sights, no sounds, no feeling. It was not an afterlife as your spirits seem to find it.

IRMA
Nothing at all? That can't be.

ARTHUR
It can be, it was. At least for me. And to be honest Irma, I've not shared this with anyone; it was what I wanted.

IRMA
Nothingness ? You wanted nothingness? That's crazy.

ARTHUR

Crazy is just a perspective.

IRMA

Craving oblivion is crazy.

ARTHUR

Life is better in the abstract; it's less messy. I think that Mick Jagger should have done a sequel to his song.

IRMA

What are you talking about?

ARTHUR

His line about getting what you need, not what you want. At the end, the true end, I think that each us of gets what we want. Most religions offer this to folks, don't you agree? They all hold out some version of Santa Claus in order to ensure compliance. (*pause*) Irma?

IRMA

I was thinking about nothing. It's not important. (*sighs*), It's nothing, continue. Go on.

ARTHUR

My next memory is of being surrounded by medical staff, what we used to call nurses. The "orderly" was nowhere to be seen. I didn't know if it had been a few seconds, or a few hours since her appearance.

IRMA

And this hadn't been a real heart attack and just an hallucination?

ARTHUR

Nope. I was discharged from the hospital later the following morning. I believe that the staff suspected that something was amiss, and wanted me out of the way, before someone else made at attempt to get me out of the way. In hindsight, it's clear that this person accidentally or deliberately killed me. I had not been on the nurses' list for any medication.

IRMA

You never pursued this angel of death? You chalked it up as a careless mistake or just another close brush with a murderer?

ARTHUR

No, I never pursued it. I was glad to be alive, and better yet, to have not suffered a heart attack.

IRMA

So oblivion can wait?

ARTHUR

Yes. Now that I know that it, that nothingness, is there, I no longer dwell on it. The over there as you call it doesn't worry me.

As far as the crime, it would have been impossible to prove. The only witness was, by his, by my own admission, dead and thus could not testify, and since, later, I was alive again, there had been no murder. Her attorney would have made me look like a fool.

All I know is that the killer didn't walk into my police station to turn herself in.

Whatever happened to Cris' husband is not dead and buried, but up in smoke. There is no case to be made.

IRMA

I don't like it, but I see your logic. No case. Oh well, I tried. *(long pause)*
And now with the afterlife, or in your case, the big void settled, you decided, at some point, to move to a town built entirely on a belief completely opposed to yours.

What are you, a missionary?

ARTHUR

I could be one with you, Irma. For a while, at least.

IRMA

Don't try to change the subject.

ARTHUR

What is the subject? We can discuss things other than spirits, you know. We can live, laugh, experience the joys of life.

IRMA

You're right of course, Arthur. Today is a beautiful day. Let's have a cool drink at my house; you can tell me more about this missionary idea of yours.

ARTHUR

I still have work to do. Let's wrap up this business with Cris. So your main complaint is that MC doesn't behave as a team player, which is bad for Rose Hill business.

IRMA

She cares only about herself. She likes the money of course.

ARTHUR

We all do. Everyone in America is a capitalist, it's the state religion.

IRMA

Maybe so, but charity is not far behind. I've helped enough people for a lifetime. She is only helping herself.

ARTHUR

Her success with clients indicates otherwise. They seem happy and satisfied.

You mentioned earlier a personal problem between you and Cris.

IRMA

What? Yes I did say that it was personal between you and "Cris"..

ARTHUR

Are you jealous of Cris?

IRMA

Of course not, she is only a psychic.

ARTHUR

That isn't what I meant. (*pause*) I'm a free agent, Irma.

IRMA

Oh, you've made that very clear.

ARTHUR

Is it a case of "If you can't have me, then on one else can"?

IRMA

I know very well what you were implying in asking me if I was jealous. If I had a case of jealousy, that was earlier. It is declinng rapidly, like a broken fever. Maybe I've become immune to it, like you being immune to shocks. I'm ready to move on, in more ways than one. You need to choose while you still have a choice..

ARTHUR

What is that supposed to mean ?

IRMA

I'll be very clear, Arthur. We are both free agents; and you would be wise to choose me, before Madame Crystal chooses you.   One way or another, a choice will be made very soon. I kept myself on the shelf for too many years, those days are over.

Life is an aphrodisiac, but it too has a short half life.

CHARLES

(*enters*) Am I disturbing you?

IRMA

Yes, but it isn't important.   Not to me, I'll leave the choice to the Sheriff. Are we through here? Its time to choose.

ARTHUR
It's not important to you, Irma?   No I guess not.   Yes. We're through. We can talk more tomorrow.

IRMA
Sure, no problem. It can wait. Like oblivion.

CHARLES
I'll only be a few minutes.

ACT II

SCENE 2

(*Sheriff's office*)

CHARLES

You and Irma appeared quite animated to me from the other the other side of the glass. I waited until there was a pause before entering.

ARTHUR

Thanks for that. Yeah, she's planning something. I can always tell.

CHARLES

It must be helpful to have a sixth sense as the sheriff in Rose Hill.

ARTHUR

You may laugh, but it is just that I have had so many dealings with people,

CHARLES

American people,

ARTHUR

Right, Americans. I recognize when they act out of character. People are people, Charles.

CHARLES

How would you know, you've met so few non-Americans. Or am I mistaken? So what is out of character with Irma?

ARTHUR

I can't put my finger on it. But I'm not going to like it. I have no illusions there.

CHARLES

Why?

ARTHUR

Because it is a change. Why do things have to change?

I envy animals; their lives are identical to those of their predecesors, millennia without change. For us, the world changes so rapidly. We do it to ourselves, as if, instead of painting ourselves in a corner, we invent and deploy technology that paints us out of our comfortable homes.

CHARLES

We are animals, too. I see the world as having two oceans, the hydrogen and the nitrogen ocean.   The air ocean and the water ocean. The birds enjoy the air ocean.

ARTHUR

While we inhabit the floor of this air ocean?

CHARLES

Yes, as sea crabs inhabit their liquid ocean.

ARTHUR

That's a pleasant thought. You've demoted me to a crab in uniform.

CHARLES

They seem more content that you do at this moment.

ARTHUR

Great. Now I get to be a crabby crab. So I'm going to crab some more. You know, I no longer recognize the country. It's out of phase.

CHARLES

Is it?

ARTHUR

It's the small items that change, those ingredients that constitute a culture. They change the most; the stone monuments themselves remain unaltered. They sit there, undisturbed as they become irrelevant. They only serve as reminders of how things used to be.

CHARLES

And you are one of these stone monuments?

ARTHUR

Well, I do feel stiff as one some mornings. I don't want to understand all of these changes. Like that tattooed woman from the séance. She should be in a carnival as an exhibit, not here in the audience. She's not the first, nor the last, I get that. Its like an incoming tide. I want to ignore it, but I can't. It's not the tattoo, by itself it is harmless. It is what the tattoo represents.

CHARLES

Which is what? Personal choice?

ARTHUR

No.

CHARLES

Freedom of expression?

ARTHUR

No. Well yes to both of those, but more basic than either of those is

CHARLES

Art?

ARTHUR

No, darn it. It represents change without reason. Unncessary change.

CHARLES

It does? Even a butterfly tattoo? You exagerrate. You are searching for something, anything, to support your view of a world changing for the worse.

ARTHUR

Have you seen American television recently? It used to be that folks confessed their sins on their deathbed, now they vaunt them as achievements, a self eulogy. When I was a kid...

CHARLES

The perfect idyllic childhood is a myth, a nonexistent golden age.

ARTHUR

I don't want to be assimilated into this new culture, this strange country that I once recognized. I've become the immigrant.

CHARLES

Everyone becomes an immigrant when they reach old age. Bizarre, we become immigrants shortly before emigrating.

ARTHUR

You've done this before, Charles. You've already emigrated. What works? Tell me.

CHARLES

I listen to the birds.

ARTHUR

I thought that Zoe did that and that you hated it.

CHARLES

I listen to their message, not their song. I see what they do and ignore what they say.

ARTHUR

Birds fly.

CHARLES

Correct.

ARTHUR

That's it?

CHARLES

That is it. But what does it mean to fly?

ARTHUR

I don't know ; I don't have a clue. I'm feeling lost in this conversation. Trees are trees and flying is flying.

CHARLES

Birds have a different perspective. I've learned from them that it is important to adopt a different perspective. We spoke the other day about the spirits of hanged men. See, I learned hanged from you, these spirits cross over the edge.

I used the word, la lisière, the edge of the forest. Treeline is perhaps the best translation.

To a bird, the tree line represents neither the barrier, nor the transition, that it does to land animals. It is not a mystery, it is nothing to fear. There is only one landscape, from the eagle's perspective, not two. From the forest the open field appears bare, desolate, but it is as full of life as under the canopy. A mon avis la lisière n'est rien du tout, alors qu'à toi, elle parait comme un grand mur.

You have unreasonable expectations, you hide in your own little forest, fearful of venturing afield.

ARTHUR

Like an old fox who knows that he can longer escape from the approaching pack of hounds.

CHARLES

An old fox, yes, that is appropriate for you.

ARTHUR

We're not birds.

CHARLES

I know (*regretfully*). They don't have to accept constraints.

ARTHUR

We are more than just birds.

CHARLES

There isn't anything more than that. There is nothing greater than birds. You share the arrogance of most humans. Sorry, it is just my perspective, my reality.

ARTHUR

Your credible lie.

CHARLES

Yes. Civilization is built on lies. And yours is your job. Is that why retirement is such a big step for you? Are you proud of what you have accomplished?

ARTHUR

I doubt that I've accomplished anything.

CHARLES

Proud, then, of what you've done?

ARTHUR

It served to pass the time.

CHARLES

That's defeatist.

ARTHUR

I'm defeated, or at least I feel defeated more and more frequently. You will be defeated too, my not so young friend; we are neither of us birds. I've done my bit, but stopping now.... I am fearful that I'd be throwing it all away. That is was a waste of time and effort. I'm hesitant to leave, and afraid to stay.

CHARLES

You, afraid?

ARTHUR

A more appropriate word doesn't spring to mind, neither in English nor in French. Afraid will have to do.

Do Frenchmen discuss topics like this between themselves? Your personal lives?

We American men get together to discuss that which we can't change, whereas women are more logical, more practical. I only realized that recently. It took a woman to teach me.

CHARLES

I haven't heard it expressed that way before. Do men underestimate women? Sure, but not myself nor anyone that I consider....

ARTHUR

Sophisticated?

CHARLES

It will do. I don't underestimate women.

ARTHUR

Not even Zoe?

CHARLES

I used to.   When she was younger, as recently as a year ago, our thoughts were different, one from another. To be candid, Zoe had none.

ARTHUR

No thoughts of her own?

CHARLES

No thoughts of her own. But now, her ideas are in sync with mine. Ironically, in coming to think like me, she has become independent. She wants to do as she pleases.
    I don't think that I underestimate her now. I wonder if I need to reconsider?

ARTHUR

I would have said the same thing about myself an hour ago. (*pause*) I/m still defined by my job. I tried to make it otherwise, when I first retired, but it didn't work out.. Its my game, or at least it was. Other people no longer respect the game and this has devalued the sport for me.

CHARLES

Life is a game. For you, your career is your life. You are playing career instead of playing life. It is an American sickness. Americans suffer a few maladies that are rare in other parts of the world. I may not have succumbed to it, but I understand its symptoms.

ARTHUR

But you did work, you played career. Everyone does.

CHARLES

I did not play it at the same elevated level as you.

ARTHUR

And now?

CHARLES

You've caught me. I still work a bit, I've been corrupted by your workaholic society.

ARTHUR

Don't tell me that you are psychic. That would be unbearable. It would represent the waste of a good man.

CHARLES

I do private placement, informally. Neither of us have work visa. I must follow American law.

ARTHUR

And that is, what, adoptions?

CHARLES

No, it is nothing like that. This village attracts folks who are open to uncoventional ideas

ARTHUR

Unconventional? That is a polite way of putting it.

CHARLES

I offer my services as a life coach.

ARTHUR

Life coach?

CHARLES

Yes. Most folks here work as death coaches, they help clients look backward.

ARTHUR
With the goal of the client moving forward....

CHARLES
If you say so. I simply bypass that step. I help... clients... you understand that I don't accept payment from them. Our visas don't permit that. I help these clients progress in their career.

ARTHUR
That sounds like difficult work (*mockingly*), Charles. Don't let it overwhelm you with stress. Life coach. Hah! Life is a game without winners, only players.

CHARLES
No, I do not agree. It is exhilarating. It focuses the mind. You Americans are always preparing for and imagining some unrealistic, better future. You don't experience the present and miss the real future. Learn to enjoy the moment. The future is overrated.

ARTHUR
It's as if I wake each day to discover that people around me are speaking a foreign language.

CHARLES
You too ? I feared that it was only me who felt that way. You are becoming an immigrant in your own country.

ARTHUR
That describes it perfectly. The so called melting pot is cold, we are, so many of us, isolated like stars in the frigid night sky.

CHARLES
But they shine, brilliantly.

ARTHUR
Without warmth.

CHARLES

And the constellations?

ARTHUR

Those are fantasies created by ancient Greeks who had no televisions. And the real immigrants, Zoe among them, are catching up to this changed society, I am falling behind. For immigrants it is an immersion class. They are assimilating, while I'm disassimilating, if that is even a word.

CHARLES

And of course, this disturbs you. You see yourself becoming obsolete, irrelevant.

ARTHUR

Yes. But it is worse than what you describe. Age makes everyone irrelevant, it makes us all disappear. No, the worst is that it is erasing my identity as an American.

Less so in Rose Hill, where nostalgia is a subtext. Even in July, this town is frozen. It advances not at all, or at only a glacial pace.

CHARLES

Rose Hill is just a layover, a relay point. Even individual spirits eventually move on. Or so it seems to me. Or else the living relations no longer come to visit. They've said their final farewells. It's only question of who does the final wave, the living or the dead. That is the real, underlying power of Rose Hil ; it is like an airport. You can't fly to Paris from just anywhere, you have to fly to Paris from a large airport.

ARTHUR

And Rose Hill is such an airport? It's is some sort of psychic hub ?

CHARLES

Yes, that is how I see it. And if your loved ones want to see you off on your flight, they come to the airport. They come to Rose Hill.

ARTHUR

I've never thought of it that way before. Be that as it may, Is that why you are here, to connect with spirits?

CHARLES

I like the birds. (*pause*) So you are losing your identity as an American?

ARTHUR

Yes.

CHARLES

There is more to being than being American.

ARTHUR

Not for me there isn't. For you it is birds, for me it is my nationality. You will think this ridiculous, but for we Americans, it is as if the world began in 1776. Anything before that is unimportant.

CHARLES

Irrelevant?

ARTHUR

Yes, absolutely.

CHARLES

That's crazy. Arrogant surement, and yes crazy.

ARTHUR

You're the second person to call me crazy in the past 24 hours, Charles.

CHARLES

It is not the correct word, I meant..

ARTHUR

That's fine. I'll accept crazy. I used to think that all of us, that we..

CHARLES

We?

ARTHUR

Sorry, that we Americans all shared one belief. The belief that we were first, last, and only Americans.

CHARLES

Franchement, Arthur, your words make me afraid. American above being human, above a religion.

ARTHUR

Not above, but equal to. To be American is to be fully human, that America is a religion.

CHARLES

And by extension, any change is heresy. I see now why you are not happy. And yet to equate being fully human with being American, that thought line leads to

ARTHUR

It doesn't need to lead anywhere other than where we are now. Other countries are proud of and don't hesitate to preserve their culture. We should do the same here.

CHARLES

Your son speaks with tree spirits that have Indian names. I don't know specifics but from what he indicated, some of them are older than your American revolution. They don't have American names. And to the original inhabitants who lost everything. History is the repeated story of "Je suis venu m'emparer de tous vos biens. Dieu est d'accord avec moi". It is a dangerous world. Living in Rose Hill does not make the world any less dangerous

In the America that I see, the only constant is change. You need to release the past like an angler releases a fish.

ARTHUR

You may be right. I have no choice but to accept it, but no desire to like it. I'm the changee, not the changer.

CHARLES

As am I. It's all the same, field or forest. To the medium, it is also   The eagles cross from field to forest without fear, without becoming lost.

ARTHUR

If only I were an eagle.

CHARLES

Eagles aren't above eating carrion. You do whatever to survive.

ARTHUR

So be it. If only I were an eagle again.

CHARLES

Pretend. That works for me.

ACT II

SCENE 3

(Town Square of Rose Hill)

IRMA

Oh I see that you've decided to come to one of our public readings. It promises to be very exciting.

ZOE

I wanted to see for myself.

BUCK

I'm very happy that you are here this morning.

MC

I bet that you are.

BUCK

These weekly sessions have been great for Dad and Chuck, they could never agree to watch either football or soccer.   They are both fans of this. Although it's a bit sick to come here to watch others' misfortune.

MC

Misfortune is the draw of most of your mens' sports.

(Arthur and Charles arrive)

ARTHUR

Have we missed anything?

IRMA

You've missed everything, Arthur.

CHARLES

Are you not participating today, Irma ? I notice that you are not wearing one of your habitual outfits for a reading.

IRMA

No, not today. Not again ever.

VARIOUS

What? You're not? What's wrong? You can't quit.

ZOE

Is it about your husband ?

BUCK

Her husband ? Irma? I thought that you were divorced.

IRMA

Zoe, you called me a crow yesterday, and today I am crowing. Yes, I'm divorced but tomorrow I will be remarried.

MC

Is it your special client?

ARTHUR

Special client, what is a special client?

IRMA

See, you do miss everything.

MC

Her client from New York, what is his name?

IRMA

His name is Derk. Yes, he and I are marrying tomorrow, in New York.

ARTHUR

Derk? No one is named Derk. What sort of a name is 'Derk'? Charles, I think that this all an elaborate hoax. Irma, you had better hurry and change, the readings will begin shortly.

IRMA

Let them start. I have no role to play.

MC

Derk is the Belgian,

IRMA

Dutchman.

MC

Whatever, from New York. He's been seeing Irma for 6 months.

IRMA

We've been seeing each other for more than a year, since the death of his wife.

ARTHUR

Oh.

IRMA

Yes, oh.

ARTHUR

I see.

CHARLES

I'm afraid that you don't see.

ZOE

So tell us the rest of your news. You can't be done crowing.

IRMA

Derk worked for years in the brokerage business, where the moode swings between greed and fear. He has made a fortune, and he has cashed in chips.

BUCK

Derk cashed in his chips? Do you mean that he died and that he is here in spirit?

IRMA

Wake up Buck, not everyone is dead. People do live first, if they are smart.. Sorry, I didn't mean snap at you like that. I'm excited that's all.

MC

Derk retired, that is all that she meant.

IRMA

Yes. He retired, with loads of cash. He can escape the finance world with its fear and greed. And so can I, with him.

ZOE

Retirement is wise, isn't it Charles? Good for you, Irma, I mean that.

IRMA

Thanks. I believe that you do. In the future, if I want to see trees, I'll stroll through Central Park.

CHARLES

When do you leave ? It must be today if the wedding will take place tomorrow.

IRMA

Within the hour.

ARTHUR

Are you mad? What about your practice, your house, your friends, me?

IRMA

Yes, I am mad. But leaving will cure me. I was like Derk, oscillating between fear and greed. I can abandon both of them here in Rose Hill, like worn out shoes. The house will be put on the market and sold by an agent. I have the few possessions that I need here in my bag; everything else is useless ballast.

MC

And your friends?

IRMA

This is why I'm speaking with all of you now.

CHARLES

Tu vas franchir la lisière de la forêt.

ZOE

He says that you are going to cross over the treeline.

IRMA

Treeline? What does.....oh yes I understand. You French do have a way with words. Yes, I'm stepping from the trees to the open field. It's much brighter in the sunshine. I have a man who loves me, who places me first instead of his job. I get to live with the folks who are one hundred percent alive.

BUCK

You are crossing over from the over there to the over here. Cool.

IRMA

Yes. And I advise you to all do the same. I said that I wasn't conducting a reading today, and I'm not. But I want to give you my counsel. You can take it or leave it.

Escape the staleness of Rose Hill. Arthur and Charles, I'm certain that you both are trapped here. I suspect that it is ether fear or greed that restrains you in this small village. But it doesn't matter which it is. What does count is that you have imprisoned yourselves here.

ARTHUR

That's not true, at least it isn't for me.

CHARLES

Moi, non plus.

ARTHUR

I'm happy here, I can't understand why you aren't satisfied.. Do you really intend to throw everything away, without any thought?

IRMA

What did you say about denials and confessions the other day? Two sides of the same coin. You men are both strong, I admire you both, but at a certain age, even strong men behave weakly. You are fearful that you can only do what you've done before, in the past. You are resistant to change.

ARTHUR

And you are chasing change without reason. You are the one that is fearful. We all age, Irma.

IRMA

Of course we do. Every day. But I'm not dead yet. Are you?

ARTHUR

These should be private conversations, Irma.

IRMA

If that were the case, I would need to charge you. Private conversations don't usually work. Do you remember ours from yesterday?

ARTHUR

Yes, of course.

IRMA

It didn't work, did it?

ARTHUR

No. Maybe I just need more time.

IRMA

I am sorry, Arthur, but I've none to lend you. All of my remaining time is allocated. It is reserved for me and Derk. Charles, the same is true for you. You and Zoe have come to a foreign country only to isolate yourselves.

And to me that makes no sense whatsoever. This is going as I expected, my pleas are falling on deaf ears.

Crystal, you are doing well here, don't let success drive you further insane with anger and regret. And Buck, the only semi sane person here, I advise you to minimize your exposure to the toxicity of this town.

                                    MC
You're reading us your last will and testament, which is nothing but insults and platitudes. Is that what you bequeath to those whom you call friends? I've better things to do, just go away.

                                    IRMA
It's evident that I've wasted precious time here, in speaking like this to you.

I look around friends, yes friends, and from your reactions, it is as if my words had been uttered in Swahili.

(*final look around, shakes her head and exits*)

                                    ARTHUR
She'll be back within a week.

                                    CHARLES
I doubt it.

                                    ARTHUR
You sound certain.

                                    CHARLES
I know people.

                                    MC
Well, Zoe, with the "great medium" married off, that leaves two attractive and available witches in town. Our odds have improved immensely.

ZOE

Speak for yourelf.

MC

Darn, I need to rush and change for my reading. If I'd known that Irma was going to ramble on like that, I'd have come in costume. At least now I'm the star of the show. (*exits*)

ZOE

(*to self*) One witch, not two. Oh how I wish that they still burned witches in this country. (*to Charles*) Irma has given us something to think about. Do you see now what I was trying to communicate to you yesterday, and the day before, and the day before that? I'm not staying for this séance after all. Charles, can we go home and discuss what she said? Please? This is more critical for us than someone's dead uncle.

CHARLES

I'm going to stay and watch it with Arthur.

ZOE

Buck, could you walk me home? (*Buck and Zoe exit*) (*drumroll*)

ARTHUR

Thank goodness that Irma shut up and left before the show began. We won't miss any of it.

CHARLES

(*sarcasm*) Yes, you don't miss anything, Arthur.

ARTHUR

Not a thing. Nor do you, apparently.

CHARLES

Irma (*pause*)

ARTHUR

Yes, what about Irma?

CHARLES

What she said, really how she spoke, how she seemed to come back to life and take control of it

ARTHUR

Hurry Charles, they're about to start.

CHARLES

Irma, is she what you meant by "a one drink woman", Sheriff?

FIN

Only Stupid Birds Sing

A play in 2 acts

By Gregory John Ferris

CHARACTERS

Charles
French, long time criminal who has never been arrested. Living in the US for less than 3 years. Resides with his girlfriend Zoe in a small rural community of psychics and spiritualists in Rose Hill in central Pennsylvania. Maintains a low profile while running a background check business for criminal clients. Enjoys walks in the nearby forests and watching birds of prey.

Zoe
French, much younger companion of Charles and, as a very effective medium, assists with his enterprise. She is seeking a normal life without Charles.

Arthur
American, middle aged, widower, sheriff. Long time law enforcement, who has found a pleasant niche in the town of Rose Hill. Has a very easy going manner, but has much experience with real criminals. Very attuned to the needs of policing in a small town, where odd is normal, and where the tourists outnumber the residents. Carries his revolver hidden in order to not appear threatening. Enjoys finer things in life, e.g. goldwasser schnapps, and has a working knowledge of French

Buck
Youngish son of Sheriff Arthur. Sole proprietor of a small logging company that contracts with an out of state baseball bat manufacturer. Enjoys bird watching and nature, and sees his vocation as managing the forest with its inhabitants, i.e. animals and the tree spirits, the latter whom he knows by name.

Romantically interested in Zoe. Shares Charles' interest in bird watching. Neither sophisticated nor a rustic.

Reno

American, early 30s, FBI agent who has been assigned to work with Elise. He has worked with psychics in the past in previous criminal cases, remains a sceptic.

Madame Crystal

Chris Burns, American. Recent arrival to Rose Hill. Originally from Chicago, she used to teach French, but now supports herself as Madame Crystal, a Hungarian Psychic, not a medium. Attracted to strong, confident men, to counterbalance the many clients that she sees as needy and weak. Has a true gift. She pursues both Arthur, and, more recently Charles.

Elise

French, 30ish, detective with Interpol who is on the track of a murder for hire organization. She believes that Charles and his companion are part of this criminal activity as the middlemen between the principal and the hired killer. After years of working the case, she believes that she must now stop Charles after the untimely death of her partner from cancer.

SETTING

Charles' and Zoe's residence, Madame Crystals and the Sheriff's office. Summer 1992

TIME

Act I, scene 1, mid-day, home of Charles and Zoe
Act I, scene 2, same afternoon, office of Sheriff Arthur   Arthur
Act I, scene 3, the next day, mid-morning, Charles' home
Act I, scene 4, a few hours later, Charles' home
Act I, scene 5, 30 minutes later, reading room of Madame Crystal
Act I, scene 6, the same time as scene 5, Charles's home

Act II, scene 1, morning, the next day, Sheriff's office
Act II, scene 2, around the same time, Charles'
Act II, scene 3, a few hours later, Charles' home

ACT I

SCENE 1

(*Residence of Charles and Zoe. Entry door stage right, bedrooms and the rest of the small house are off stage left. The room is decorated with photos of birds of prey and little else. Near stage left is a small table with 2-4 chairs*)

CHARLES
(*Speaking to a person, not seen, on the other side of the open entry door*)
Well, I have your contact information...Yvonne. If the agency is interested, they will contact you in a few days, by phone, at this number (*holding business card*).

YVONNE
And you can't give me any information on the client?

CHARLES
(*Smiling*) I'm sorry Yvonne, but I don't know that myself. I simply perform the background check, as I mentioned, sorry. Good luck.

YVONNE
Thanks again.

CHARLES
(*Closes door and turns stage left where Zoe is entering*) Alors, que penses-tu d'elle? So, what do you think Zoe?

ZOE
(*hesitant*) I'm not sure, she is...

CHARLES

(*goes from happy to exasperated*) Trop quoi? Too what? Too young, too old, too tall, too French? Or not French enough, because she is Canadienne?

ZOE

(*hesitant*) She is just not correct for this assignment. Something in the way she moves..

CHARLES

Oh, not again. Don't quote McCartney. He's not Sartre, you know. Look, we have to make a decision on this posting. We must be current with the times. What is the word, yes, diversity, or is it diversify. Yes, we need some diversity. You know as well as I that our customers ask us to send to them candidates who can bring special abilities to their business endeavors. They no longer want the same type of candidates as before. It's a new fashion, perhaps, but we need to accept that this is the style of today.

(*regards card again*)

This, Yvonne, the Canadienne. She is comfortable with both English and French, and is very persistent, you heard that yourself just minutes ago. She is pretty, too.

ZOE

That must be what I noticed. She is overly pretty for this opening. Someone like her would be too noticeable, a distraction.

CHARLES

How can you say that? You don't know. These postings in the Journal are never that detailed. This one wasn't. Listen (*reads aloud*),

« Searching English/French speaking woman for assignment in a remote, rural environment. Must be a self-starter and persistent. Ability to easily blend in a plus. »

Where does it say that she must not be attractive

ZOE

Well, with those 4 inch heels, she certainly wouldn't blend in here. And if you look out the window I'm sure that she has attracted every single man within scent of her Chanel.

CHARLES

Perhaps you are correct this time. And yet her background check was impeccable, you said so yourself.

ZOE

I know that I did, but....

CHARLES

Ok, you win Cherie. But the next French speaker who passes your examination will receive this assignment. I don't care if she walks in here nude...

ZOE

Yes, you would.

CHARLES

Zoe, you know what I intended to say. We are 10 hours from Quebec. Even Pittsburgh is over 3 hours by car. French speakers are not exactly dropping from the billion trees that surround us in this outpost of the bizarre called Rose Hill.

ZOE

I'm part of that bizarreness. Maybe the most bizarre. La crème de la crème, you called me once. Spoiled cream now. Living this remotely was your idea; remote but accessible by the great Interstate 80 that stretches from coast to coast. Anyone with a car can turn up for an interview. Remember, Charles? The best of both worlds. So you said.

CHARLES

Yes, of course. I am sorry, forgive me Zoe. It's just that this job opening won't last forever. We have turned away so many valid prospects. (*tries to lighten the situation*) If I didn't know better Cherie, I would say that you want this assignment for yourself. Are you thinking of changing careers?

ZOE

(*smiles weakly*)   I would not pass the background check.

CHARLES

(*laughs*) Not yours. But believe me, you're qualified. You may not have pulled the trigger or slipped in the poison, but you know very well how it is done, how it has been done. (*looks at a photo of a young eagle flying*) I was thinking of you when I snapped this photograph.

Zoe, you are a young eagle who has dined on raw meat often enough. You want to soar and swoop by yourself. I see it in your eyes. (*laughs and pauses*).

That is one of the few, non-financial, benefits of residing in this village; the raptors are ever present. I feel at home here sometimes.

ZOE

Charles, you may be a better judge of me than I am of myself. Yes, you know me well. I am ready for a change.   But, d'accord, OK, I will agree to this. The next French speaking woman who walks through that door will be given the assignment.

CHARLES

Provided that she passes the background check.

ZOE

Of course. Provided that she passes. (*pauses*)   That Canadienne, Yvonne, was exhausting. Her resume was so full of recent activity that I'd have thought that she needed a vacation instead of another job. The clients from the other side were queued up.

CHARLES

No rest for the wicked was never more true.

ZOE

She is a very nasty individual.

CHARLES

That is the exactly the sort of person that we provide. She excels at nasty. She is still a no?

ZOE

Yes, she remains a no. By the way, it was George and not Paul who wrote « Something ».

CHARLES

I must be slipping. Yes, George Harrison. I knew that. I should have known better. Mistakes can be deadly.

ZOE

This talk of death, will it never end with us?

CHARLES

Death is a good living.

ZOE

(*Pause*) Are you going bird watching with Buck again today?

CHARLES

Bird watching? You make it sound weak.

ZOE

It is weak, isn't it? Just staring at birds through binoculars.

CHARLES

The birds are magnificient, they are not silly songbirds. These raptors are natural killers; they lack remorse. Like you. Aren't they?

ZOE

(*weak smile*) Of course. Killers. Like us.

CHARLES

Its not all sitting and watching; its exercise and relaxation at the same time.

I need to change into my hiking boots and fetch my camera...and binoculars.

ZOE

Put on a heavier shirt as well, Charles. (*kisses Charles on cheek, before he exits stage left*)

(*Knock at door, Buck enters*):

BUCK

Hi Zoe. Is Chuck ready? I came a few minutes early. To see you.

ZOE

He's changing into his hiking gear. He will be a while as I knotted his boots.

BUCK

(*rapidly approaches Zoe and kisses her*) I'll make sure to extend the hike so that he returns exhausted. Let's meet at 8 o'clock tonight at the regular spot. Will you be there, Zoe?

ZOE

(*looks over shoulder stage left*) Yes. OK. Just remember Buck, that Charles is very possessive, don't talk too much when you two are together.

BUCK

No danger of that, Chuck doesn't ever say much.

ZOE

You're the only one that calls him that; I doubt that he would permit anyone else to refer to him as Chuck. He tolerates your nickname, je ne sais pourquoi. But I am telling you to be circumspect, don't blabber on to him. With Charles there is always danger. You must be discreet.

BUCK

O (*pause*) K (*pause*) is that good?

ZOE

Perfect (*quick kiss*)

BUCK

Have you told him yet about us?

ZOE

No, not yet.

BUCK

When, Zoe?

ZOE

When, What, Why? All of these short questions that demand such long answers.

BUCK

They do? Today, tomorrow, either of those is a short enough answer for me.

ZOE

Charles needs me.

BUCK

I do too. I need you even more than he does. You said the word danger a moment ago. Has he hurt you?

ZOE

No… maybe.

BUCK

What?

ZOE

No, I mean that I, that he and I often hurt each other. It is as if we cannot help ourselves. We can be like two animals in a small cage. But we throw only words at each other He injures me only with words, Buck.

BUCK

Let's leave, right this minute. Just walk out the door with me.

ZOE

I can't, not yet. Charles and I are tied together like the laces of his stupid boots. I wish that I could unlace him from me. Or simply slice through them.

BUCK

It's not a marriage knot. Even if it were...

ZOE

He and I still need each other.

BUCK

Still? That means until when?

ZOE

We have circled back to that simple question, to when.

BUCK

He doesn't value you as I do. (*noises from stage left*)

ZOE

Soon. A few days.

(*Charles reenters stage left, wearing boots, new shirt, binoculars and a camera, and a ball cap*).

BUCK

Hey Chuck.

CHARLES

(*winces at the name Chuck, then smiles*) Hey Buck.

ZOE

(*laughs*) Voila. Le touriste français. Très drôle.

BUCK

Touriste Yes, quite the tourist, Chuck.

ZOE

Even the name (*laughs again*), Chuck.

BUCK

Well it won't be long now. I saw those eaglets again, they were making the typical preflight motions. They are going to leave the nest soon.

CHARLES

(*looking at Zoe*) That is what eaglets do; they soar on their own. How soon? How soon, Zoe?

ZOE

How would I know? I know nothing of eagles, except that they are killers.

CHARLES

(*turns to Buck*) Soon?

BUCK

Yes, I think that it will be very soon. It may even happen this afternoon. Are you interested in riding up there with me; we might see their first solo.

CHARLES

I'm happy to see that you are feeling better, Zoe. Rest while we're gone in any case. (*fiddling with gear and looking down*) Buck, what do you think about parking the car near that one large hemlock tree, what do you call it? That way there will be little risk of disturbing the raptors.

BUCK

O (*pause*) K (*winks at Zoe*). It will still require a long hike. Is that good?

CHARLES

Yes, that sounds perfect.

BUCK

Kittana.

CHARLES

Kittana what ?

BUCK

The large hemlock is named Kittana. You'd asked me her name.

CHARLES

Is that your name for her, or the tree's name?

BUCK

She. She calls herself Kittana.

CHARLES

(*speaking aloud to all and no one*) I love this town. I truly do. After two year it continues to surprise me with its oddity. Between the dozens of psychics, mediums, spiritualists, you Buck are one of the few, perhaps the sole inhabitant who only communicates with trees.Your career as a woodsman makes it even more paradoxical.

BUCK

Not really, Chuck. You know, of course, that the sheriff is my father. People always ask me why I didn't follow him into law enforcement.

ZOE

I wondered that. You never told me, told us why you became a lumberjack. Why not join the police?

BUCK

I did.

CHARLES

(*shocked*) The police! You're a flic? (*Pause*) A cop?

BUCK

(*laughing*) Don't worry. I'm not going to arrest you for bird watching, Chuck.

I meant police in another sense. I police the forest. You may think this insane.

CHARLES

(*relieved*) Insane? In Rose Hill? Impossible. How would you be able to distinguish the rational from the irrational? Lunacy is the defining characteristic of this village.

BUCK

Lunatic or not, I police the forest. Not all of the tree spirits are good, you know. Or maybe not. No, you probably don't know. But some of these tree spirits are real jerks, they mistreat the other trees, they are only in it for themselves. Those are those ones that most often make it to my mill, and from there into baseball bats. The woods may appear peaceful, but it can be a violent world; there, the weak can't retreat as folks can do here. It is a silent war. The trees are rooted in place. People can pack up and leave, or simply leave.

ZOE

So there are both good and bad trees? Inside, I mean. Not diseased or malformed, but bad? Evil? Trees have spirits?

BUCK

Of course trees have spirits. You should trust me on this Zoe, I know what I am doing. The trees with evil spirts are not malformed visibly such that you Zoe or you Chuck would notice it. Both of you are ordinary (*pause*), sorry, I should say normal. You're not sensitive. (*pause*) Sorry again, don't take offense. You're just not sensitive, not in the way that I am.

CHARLES

I can agree with that. We are not at all similar in that respect, if any. Believe me, I'm not offended.

BUCK

Good. Anyway some of the best trees are also the worst. Great for construction but poorly constructed.

ZOE

(*turns away, to herself*) Great life, but bad for the living. Spoiled cream.

BUCK

What was that?

ZOE

Nothing. Have a good time.

Charles and Buck exit stage right. Zoe looks at the photo for 30 seconds and then turns and begins walking stage left. Doorbell rings. Zoe, stops, pauses, and continues stage left. Doorbell rings again. Zoe, turns around and walks slowly to answer door.
Madame Crystal enters, Hungarian accent

MADAME CRYSTAL (MC)

Hello Zoe, is Charles in? I was out walking earlier and found this feather. I'm sure that it is from a hawk, or perhaps even an eagle. Finding one is a very good sign, being so psychically connected, I know all about signs. I thought that we could have coffee, Charles and me that is, and he could determine which species this is from. You look completely worn out Zoe. So, is Charles at home?

ZOE

(*Cold*) No. Charles is definitely not available Madame..

MC

Zoe, just call me Crystal. There is no need to use my title behind closed doors. Madame Crystal is really just for my clients.

ZOE

I was going to say Madame Mesmer. Isn't that your married name?

MC

(*surprised*) Who told you that?

ZOE

Buck. His father, Sheriff Arthur, must have mentioned it to him.

MC

I'm not married, not now. I reverted to using my maiden name after the death of my husband. So Arthur, the sheriff, researched my background. He and I are having dinner later, what better topic can there be to discuss than me.

ZOE

He's thorough. He has time to investigate.

MC

Hmm, so Arthur was checking on me. It is to be expected, of course. A good looking, available woman moves into a small town. All of the players pay attention.

ZOE

Players?

MC

That would include all of the single men who have any sense. Even some of the married men. They're players. It's only natural that they notice me.

ZOE

Folks notice road kill around here too. The ones who stop to pick it up aren't the sensible ones. As I said, Charles is not here.

MC

He is not with that blonde friend of yours is he?

ZOE

Blond friend? He is bird watching with Buck, and he is certainly not blond.

MC

I was referring to the young, blonde woman that I saw leaving here earlier. She was really something, very attractive. Someone to die for, as they say today. Don't you agree? (*no response*). She was dressed as for an interview. She's a friend of yours?

ZOE

Blonde woman? Oh, her. No, she is not a friend.

MC

Not a friend of yours? (*Jealous*) A friend of Charles'?

ZOE

An acquaintance of the both of us. She was just passing through on her way back home

MC

To Québec.

ZOE

Yes, Québec. How did you know?   (*drily*) Oh that's right, you are Madame Mesmer

MC

(*angrily*) Madame Crystal. I guessed that she was your «friend » and so I figured that she must speak French. I said bonjour to her and we spoke in French for a few minutes.

ZOE

(*distracted and disturbed by this news*) Really. I wasn't aware that you spoke the language.

MC

It's been a while, I taught it for many, a few years in…

ZOE

Chicago.

MC

Yes, Chicago. Buck certainly keeps you… filled…… with information.

ZOE

And so these so call language lessons with Charles, they are not necessary…

MC

I'd classify them as a refresher. I certainly feel refreshed afterwards. Your Buck does talk too much, but strangely, he is very quiet about you two.

ZOE

Charles and I keep to ourselves. He has his hobbies and I have..

MC

You and Charles are not the two that I meant. And you have what, or who, here in….?

ZOE

We should start a French club in Rose Hill. Between you and I and…

MC

Why haven't you registed?

ZOE

others who may be interested. Especially since you speak it so well. Charles wouldn't mind sharing you; there seems to be a lot of you to go around.

MC

You are required to register, you know.

ZOE

Register a French club? You're not serious. I thought that America had freedom of speech.

MC

No.

ZOE

No? I am certain that..

MC

You are supposed to, required to register with the town council as a psychic.

ZOE

I don't understand.

MC

You do understand. Zoe, you have a wonderful was of appearing to not comprehend. We can have our first French club meeting here, now. Je sais ce que tu fait. How's that?

ZOE

I still don't know what you want to tell me. Ou voulez-vous en venir ?

MC

That young lady, so well dressed, tirée à quatre épingles, told me that she had come to see you for a reading. A reading. You need to be registered if you want to do readings.

This may even be against your visa restrictions. You're not permitted to work.

ZOE

Readings are work? I thought that you performed them as a service, a vocation. I must have been misinformed: no freedom of speech, no freedom of religion in America?

MC

You can be nasty, Zoe.

ZOE

When it is required. (*pause*) Coming from you, I consider that as a sign of professional respect. The blonde, she was just joking, she is like that. In any case, being « Hungarian » how are you able to work?

MC

What is her name?

ZOE

Her name? (*pause and turns away*) She did not tell it to you? (*spots Yvonne's card on table and reads and hides it in pocket*)

MC

She did.

ZOE

It's likely that she created a fake name on the spot; she is always joking. Something Hungarian, I'd expect (*laughs*)

MC

What is her name?

ZOE

Arthur does the investigations in this town, not you Crystal. Anyway, you should be able to tell me her real name. You are the psychic, not me.

MC

I'm not so sure.

ZOE

(*tired of fencing*) Her name is Yvonne. Satisfied?

MC

For now. I'll stop by another time to visit with Charles. Now, I need to confirm reservations for dinner tonight with Arthur. (*turns to leave*)

ZOE

(*again on the attack*) It does not require a psychic to see that he is not interested in you.

MC

Arthur? Believe me Zoe, he is interested. I just told you twice that we are having dinner, again, tonight. Sure he is interested. Arthur is a player.

ZOE

He is certainly playing you, Crystal. Take my advice and pass on dinner; it will be an interrogation with dessert.

MC

An interrogation? Even if it is, I have nothing to hide.

ZOE

Crystal, we all have something to hide, if not from him, then from ourselves.

MC

That is very good, do you use that line during your readings?

ZOE

I'll repeat what I said earlier; I don't do readings.

MC

Very well, then. This visit has not been a complete waste. I will add your line about hiding from ourselves to my repertoire. The tourists really seem to relish meaningless phrases like that one.

ZOE

I meant Charles.

MC

Charles?

ZOE

(*calmly*) Yes, It is Charles who has no interest in you. He is with me. Stay away.

MC

(*mocking laugh*) He may be with you, today, for now. But are you with him?

ZOE

(*done with fencing for the second time*) I am tired, épuisée. If you will excuse me (*guiding MC to door, without touching her*).

MC

Sure, Zoe. I'm leaving. Readings tire us all. (*exits stage right*)

ZOE

(*a final long look at the eagle photo and then slowly exits stage left*)

ACT I

SCENE 2

(*Public area and waiting room, i.e. one common room for sheriff's business, Agent Elise Gaar and Special Agent Reno are planning their upcoming meeting with Sheriff Arthur. A few chairs along the wall as well as a desk with two facing chairs*)

ELISE

How much longer will it be? The sign indicated that he would be back by 4 PM. It is later than that now.

RENO

What is the hurry, we won't start until tomorrow. You need to rest more than anything. After the flight from Paris and the long drive here, you must be in a fog.

ELISE

I don't know how much time remains for me.

RENO

I've been in the same situation many times myself. There is always something more pressing. I jump from state to state and case to case as I'm sure you do. How many days has Interpol given you to finish this one?

ELISE

This case? I've been on this case for years now. But I can see the time ticking away. This is my best chance. Time is the only variable.

RENO

Oh, I misunderstood. You've been assigned to this investigation for years? Wow. It must be huge. Isn't it unusual for an agent to pursue supects alone? I know that your longtime partner, Guy (*not sure of name*) died, but surely you've been provided another.

ELISE
There hasn't been time. Guy passed away only 2 days ago. I had to leave Paris immediately.

RENO
You couldn't stay for the funeral? That seems callous.

ELISE
The case is too big, we'd been on it for so long, that I couldn't let death get in the way. Guy understood. We knew that the job comes first.

RENO
OK. Good luck in finding another partner, with that attitude. I hope that you sent flowers. Or would that have been a distraction as well?

ELISE
We said our goodbyes beforehand. He died from a cancer, it wasn't job related.

RENO
I bet that he was glad to know that, a job related death would have been so disappointing to him.

ELISE
Reno, I recognize sarcasm. It was cancer, a medical villain that killed Guy. Neither of us could stop it. Many educated people are on his trail--- cancer I mean. Guy and I weren't, aren't that smart, we are reduced to chasing human villains. I didn't apologize to Guy for continuing this hunt, and I assuredly do not intend to apologize to you.

RENO
I got it Elise. Message received. We can stop the bad cop/bad cop routine when its just the two of us.

                              ELISE
OK.

                              RENO
So you and Guy have been after this Frenchman, Charles for two years.

                              ELISE
No, four years. He has been living in the states for two years.

                              RENO
Obviously, I am not current with all aspects of your four year investigation, but surely it is even more difficult now that Charles is living outside of France, and without the aid of Guy.

                              ELISE
I expect that it will easier without Guy here. That is the entire essence of my plan. And why time is so precious.

                              RENO
Do you mean the Guy slowed you down because of his illness?

                              ELISE
Not really, he…

                              RENO
Was he crooked? Corrupt?

                              ELISE
(*a bit angry*) No, he...

                              RENO
So the mob doesn't know that Guy is dead and you have a double, a Guy look-alike on the way? That must have required some surgery, maybe fake fingerprints..

                              ELISE
(*still angry*) Don't be silly, he..

RENO

So Guy is not dead after all, but he is corrupt and he has given you enough to trap Charles?

ELISE

(*silent, ignores Reno*)

RENO

Elise? (*pause*) Elise? (*pause*) Say something

ELISE

(*puts her hand over the mouth of Reno*) Silence. I will speak now. Why do you ask questions and then interrupt my answers? No, remain silent. That is no way to have a conversation. The interrogation rooms, if they exist in this so called Sheriff's office, are in the back, not here in this waiting room. (*removes hand from Reno's mouth and leans back*).

Guy is dead. You know nothing of him. He was not corrupt. Let's play good cop/ good cop when it is just us. Isn't that what you suggested?

RENO

Sorry, I did not mean to accuse your late partner of anything. I'm sure that he was, (*pause*), no, as you indicated, I know nothing of him. In fact, I'm more confused now than I was 10 minutes ago.

ELISE

How is that?

RENO

I took a flight from Seattle to Washington, DC, for a briefing on this. A briefing that can only be described as absurd. This was followed by some Thai food that was just as absurd, then a flight to JFK to meet you. And finally, we had the very long drive here. You were able to sleep a bit in the car, not much as you appeared quite agitated. You still do. We are both tired, we can't really do anything until the morning. Elise, we could have stopped in here at that time.

ELISE

I am sorry too, Reno. I'm excited, agitated as you said, and exhausted at the same time. If I sit much longer, I'll fall asleep. Keep talking.

RENO

Perhaps we should just check into a hotel and approach the sheriff in the morning, when we will both be fresh.

ELISE

No, no, no, no, no. I'm not sure how much time remains.

RENO

You continue to say that. (*pause*) You stated that this would be easier now without Guy. What makes it so?

ELISE

You will know that tomorrow, if I'm correct. If not, I will be on a plane back to Paris and will weep at his grave, because I will have failed. (*pause*)

(*Elise rises and goes to coffee pot and feels it*)

Good, it's cold.

RENO

Cold is good?

ELISE

Yes, with American coffee, cold is better.

RENO

Intriguing. Why is that?

ELISE

American coffee is too weak; very rarely is it strong enough for sophisticated European taste buds.

RENO

Everyone knows that.

ELISE

More sarcasm. I deserve it, this time. (*smiles*). So whenever I have a cup of hot American coffee, I am always hopeful that this time, that this cup will be wonderful.

Of course, I am almost always disappointed.

RENO

Of course. And cold?

ELISE

With cold coffee I know that there is no chance of pleasure, no hope, and donc, no disappointment.

RENO

That follows a weird sort of logic. Logic in a town that defies logic.

ELISE

According to your briefing?

RENO

Yes

ELISE

Can you share it with me?

RENO

My meeting in DC? I don't see why not. I'll share of it what I can, probably all of it. I don't recall anything being above your clearance level. Frankly, this assignment is just another organized crime case, with the psychic village setting the only oddity. A big oddity for sure.

ELISE

It is the crux of the case.

RENO

That remains to be seen. So, the bureau has sent me from the forests of Washington State to the heart of Pennsylvania's woods in order to help you trap this hit man headhunter.

ELISE

Headhunter?

RENO

It is slang for a recruiter, for an employment agency.

ELISE

Yes, I see. I am searching for a headhunter in this northern jungle. In this case a real headhunter. As far as I can determine he has over 50 murders to his « credit ».

RENO

50? I had not heard any numbers. But he is only the recruiter, correct?

ELISE

Yes, he is the recruiter. You say only the recruiter as if that reduces his guilt.

RENO

It was phrased poorly. I meant to say that he is a link, one link in a chain. Getting back to my briefing, which, to tell the truth, likely originates with you Elise, here is what I know.

Neither Charles nor Zoe has any type of criminal record, no arrests, no convictions, but plenty of suspicions in France. This comes from you, your Interpol files. In summary, whether it is two years or four years, you have nothing.

In the US, it is the same, neither has even been issued a parking ticket.

And there is not much more from my folks in D.C.

Charles has been in the US for about 2 years, all of it in Rose Hill, Pennsylvania, full time population 312. He lives here with his young girlfriend Zoe, who is not his wife. No children. They seem to live modestly, and while their bank accounts are good sized and assist in them being able to stay here in the US, they are not rich. At least as far as the bureau has found.

Neither works, they have few, if any friends. They have no fancy cars, no car at all as a matter of fact, which is unusual. That explains the lack of parking tickets, obviously (*smiles at Elise, who smiles tiredly back*). Zoe doesn't wear any expensive jewelry. She resembles a China doll that does absolutely nothing.

Charles enjoys walks in the woods, and enjoys bird watching and photography. His only close acquaintance, as I mentioned, neither Charles nor Zoe have friends, is this timber man Buck. A lumberjack with his own small company.

This is boring with a capital B. The only coincidence is that this Buck is the son of the local sheriff. In whose office we currently sit. Even that seems harmless; in a town of 312, there is not many choices for acquaintances.

                         ELISE
You have nothing else, even after an FBI briefing ?

                         RENO
Zero plus zero equals zero, Elise. In France and in America.

                         ELISE
So Charles leads a quiet life.

                         RENO
A very quiet, peaceful life. One that I might find appealing myself, if I were his age. Dull, but appealing.

Elise, if Interpol had not contacted the bureau, we would not be investigating this man. There is nowhere for him to either hide or run to. You said that he leads a quiet life. I would go further and claim that he has exiled himself here. If he were a criminal, perhaps he has sentenced himself to Rose Hill.

ELISE

Don't be fooled by appearances, Reno. Rose Hill is essential to his criminal plan. He is not retired, not laying low as they say in old movies. He has, if anything, increased his activity. This peaceful façade is just that, the illusions of a master magician.

RENO

Perhaps. And it is because you may be correct that we have been sent to this village. But, right now, there is no point in even surveilling Charles. Unless he is communicating by pigeon, he sees no one. And unless there is an eastern species of Sasquatch, that's a mythical ape, in the woods around Rose Hill, there is nothing in the surrounding forest except trees, deer, and his beloved hawks and eagles.

ELISE

OK. Agreed.

RENO

Agreed?

ELISE

Yes. That is why we need to take a more direct approach. You will go in tomorrow and try to have him hire you.

RENO

As an assassin?

ELISE

Yes, exactly.

RENO

Yes exactly, you say. Here comes some more sarcasm. Oh, that should be easy enough. I just wanted to verify that with you Elise. I was concerned that after two flights, one briefing, one bad Thai dinner, and nine hours in a government class rental car, that the plan was going to be difficult.

ELISE

Relax, my plan is simple.

RENO

So, tomorrow, I knock on Charles' door and say, good morning, I'm special agent Reno with the FBI. I saw your ad and decided to go rogue and become one of your assassins. Do you offer health benefits and a matching 401k?

ELISE

Be serious. What is a 401k? A gun?

RENO

Never mind. If it was as easy as knocking on his door, you and your partner would have captured Charles long ago.

ELISE

I said simple, not easy. I have two pieces of information. One is the advertisement of which you spoke, here it is Reno. (*Reno opens mouth to speak, Elise puts finger to her lip to silence him*). You were joking, I know, but here, read it. According to myself and Guy, and with the concurrence of the best minds of Interpol, this is an ad for murder. The FBI reviewed our documentation and agreed. That is why I am here and you are here, Special Agent Reno.

RENO

Wow. A job posting? In the newspaper? Which? The New York Journal (*laughing*)?

ELISE

(*triumphant smile*) Yes, exactly.

RENO

Stop saying that.

ELISE

Yes, exactly?

RENO

Yes, exactly. I am awake now Elise, let me try some of that cold coffee. (*Pours himself some cold coffee*). So, the bureau must have green lit this operation a while ago.

ELISE

Yes, a few weeks ago.

RENO

Its a shame that Guy died before he was able to nab this guy. Let me see the ad.

(*Reads it out loud, same as the one that Charles read*)

« Searching English/French speaking woman for assignment in a remote, rural environment. Must be a self-starter and persistent. Ability to easily blend in a plus. »

It looks innocuous, it says nothing. Just a few words and a telephone number.

ELISE

And look at this one and this one and this one. The bureau didn't show you any of these during the briefing? That's odd.

RENO

The operative word was brief. (*reading silently through a few ads*). Hey, this one is in.. French?

ELISE

Yes, French.

RENO

That's strange. The same phone number appears in all of these ads. That would be normal if it is from the same agency. Whose number is it?

ELISE

Just an answering machine, asking the caller to leave a name and a call back number. Not unusual, a typical configuration. We tried it a few times, leaving various names and numbers. We never had a response.

RENO

Interesting. And then? There has to be a « and then ».

ELISE

Yes, ex--- . Yes. And then Guy had the wonderful idea to call from a public payphone, you know that they can be identified by number. Voila. He was called back almost immediately. A few unusual questions, totally inappropriate for any legitimate agency, followed by the name Charles and this town. That was it.

RENO

That sounds like a quite a bit to me, a valid lead.

ELISE

We repeated the experiment with different voices, ads, and payphones. We received the same results: Rose Hill and Charles.

RENO

Ok. So all of this that you just explained is one part of the information to break the case. What is the second? More ads?

ELISE

No something else. Something much better, I hope, but I can't tell you. Not yet. Reno, I was briefed on you as well, at JFK, before I cleared customs.

RENO

I wondered why you took so long to disembark. As law enforcement, you should have cleared Customs immediately. So, tell me about myself.

ELISE

You have 12 years with the FBI. In the past, you worked abduction cases, in some where psychics were consulted.

RENO

Worthless! Sorry, continue.

ELISE

Let me think. Reno has a talent for the theatrical which better suits him for undercover work. He, you, switched to the organized crime unit after the resolution of several high profile abduction, during which he (you) excelled at maintaining anonymity from the general public.

Worthless?

RENO

Who, me?

ELISE

The psychics. I repeated verbatim some words that were said to me at my meeting at JFK a few hours ago. These were, "you consulted psychics during some abduction cases".

You nearly shouted « Worthless ! »

RENO

In general yes, they are worthless. These psychics are most often either fakes or fools. (*pause*). And yet in several instances, their assistance was invaluable. I was so accustomed to telling reporters, really having other agents pass the word to them, that psychics were worthless that I developed the habit. In some cases, they were a secret weapon; and there is no sense in disclosing that, either to the public or the abductors. (*pause*). Wait a minute, I know your secret weapon, this second piece of information. You've convinced the girlfriend, Zoe, to turn on Charles? She is going to betray her lover?

ELISE

No, Reno, I have not « turned » Zoe, as you put it. I've never even met her; if I had this trip would have not have been possible for me. It would have been worthless (*smiles*). I have no idea which role, if any, she plays in this macabre play. She's a cypher: orphaned to a single mother, raised by a widowed aunt who had been married to Zoe's mother's brother.

RENO

Her aunt through marriage?

ELISE

Is that the phrase, aunt through marriage? (*Pause*) Zoe took up with Charles soon after her 17th birthday. She has no formal education, no outside interests other than some mountain hiking, randonner we would say in French. She is nothing, a cypher.

RENO

Another oddball in Rose Hill. Elise, this ad calls for a woman.

ELISE

I know that you like theatrics, but you won't be performing in drag tomorrow. Relieved?

RENO

That was never my sort of theatrics.

ELISE

(*rehanding him the other ads*) Choose one or more of these clippings. (*pause*) I find it strange that the ads are precise in this regard.

RENO

Which regard?

ELISE

In the way that they describe the prospective candidates. This seems to be ameturish, almost absurd in a murder for hire organization. Maybe in isolated cases, a particular type might be required, but it seems to be a common theme in these ads.

RENO

I'll express interest in two of these to Charles tomorrow, one that clearly doesn't fit me, and one that does.

ELISE

Brilliant. Any details that you can uncover before I arrive will help my, our chances.

RENO

I'm very happy to hear that this now a joint operation.

ELISE

It has been since we met at JFK last night.

RENO

So what is this second piece of information?

ELISE

That was a nice try, Reno, but you need to wait. I cannot reveal that to you quite yet. What should we divulge to this Sheriff?

RENO

The normal. As much as we have to, and as little as possible. We are here doing a check on two French nationals for possible illegal activity. This much is true. We can imply that it involves drugs or tax evasion, but I won't lie to him. He can provide us with recent background on Charles and his circle as well as other Rose Hill inhabitants who might be relevant. This sheriff is probably the only law enforcement that has spoken with Charles in two years.

ELISE

You raise an excellent point.A great deal can happen in two years.

RENO

More than anything, this is a courtesy call; it is good manners to announce ourselves. Still, this connection between Charles and the son, Buck...that disturbs me.

ELISE

Do you think that the sheriff is involved and that Buck is the go between?

RENO

Now it is you who is jumping to conclusions. Speculation is just that. (*pause*) No, I doubt that the sheriff is involved. But we still need to consider this possibility. He or his son. Quiet, here he comes.

SHERIFF ARTHUR

(*enters, simple uniform, no handcuffs, no gun. Just a badge and a hat*) Howdy folks. I hope that you haven't been waiting long. Good, so what can I do for you?

(*Introductions*)

(*Sheriff goes to turn open/closed sign on door, does not lock it, when he sees who they are as they present their ids. Returns to his desk*).

ARTHUR

The FBI and Interpol. Are you two lost? Broken down on Interstate 80? (*pause*). No, assuredly not. Agent Elise Gaar of Interpol and Special Agent Reno of the FBI. Is that RENO like the city or RENO like the French actor?

RENO

I answer to both, Sheriff.

ARTHUR

And agent Gaar. Bienvenue a Rose Hill Madame l'agent.

ELISE

(*flabbergasted*) Parlez-vous francais monsieur le commissaire?

ARTHUR

Je me debrouille. (*to Reno*). I manage, I get by. Folks, just call me Arthur, I run a very informal, and small, department. (*looks at IDs again*) May I call you Elise?

ELISE

Of course, Arthur.

ARTHUR

No first name, Reno?

RENO

Nope, just Reno, Arthur.

ARTHUR

I had too much coffee at lunch, give me two minutes and I will be able to focus on whatever it is that you want to discuss. (*leaves with IDs, exit stage left*)

ELISE

Reno, you may be right.

RENO

I am?

ELISE

I cannot believe that this Sheriff speaks French. Perhaps he is the carrier pigeon of which you spoke. Who would be better placed to provide cover for Charles' crimes than the local police?

RENO

He seems straight forward enough at first glance. I'm not convinced that he or anyone has committed a crime on US soil. In fact, he reminds me of that old TV show.

ELISE

Do all Americans see the world as a TV show, are those your only cultural references ?   Never mind, it's not important, my thoughts are jumbled and this Sheriff adds to my confusion.

RENO

Why, what has he done?

ELISE

Two special agents are in his office, and he needs to run to the toilet. I find that suspicious.

RENO

You do? I've only had half a cup of this marvelous cold police coffee and I may need to follow his example.

ELISE

Put youself in his place.   Would you have left?   We came here specifically to see him, to his office. And he bolts like a rabbit. Would you have done that ?

RENO

No, I guess not.   I don't like this at all.   It is just another unlikely coincidence on top of his son and Charles being buddies. We might be on to something big, Elise.

ELISE

We?

RENO

It is a joint operation.

ARTHUR

(*returns*) That is much better. Oh, here are your credentials back. So, what brings two of the world's best detectives to Rose Hill? I still can't believe it, Interpol and the FBI in Rose Hill. Just wait until my boy hears about this. This really calls for a drink. (*looks warily Elise and Reno*).

No objection if I have one? (*Elise and Reno shake their heads*). (*He pulls a bottle of Goldwasser from the desk and pours himself a wine glass's worth.*)

Attendez

This is my own crystal ball. I got the idea from one of the psychics years ago. He died a while back, so I don't feel guilty using his technique. (*Elise and Reno exchange glances during this process*).   See how these flakes of gold float? They speak to me.

I see that you have both come on a long voyage. Yes, far from these deep, dark woods. You are seeking my help. You are intent on capturing one, no two, these flakes really shine, don't they, two fugitives from Europe. Yes Europe, but wait, what does the gold whisper, no not just Europe, but France. I see bird feathers. And a couple. I can't see a name, the flakes are twisting too much, but (*drinks and swallows the goldwasser*). (pause) Ah. It is clear now. Certainly, you search Charles and Zoe. (*long pause*)

(*Arthur laughs loudly*):   You should see your expressions. (*laughs again*) How do you like my shtick? I have so many role models here in Rose Hill from which to choose. (*pause*) Relax kids, I am not a psychic.

ELISE
That is reassuring Arthur, I was concerned for a moment. Why do you mention this Charles and Zoe? Who are they?

ARTHUR
Charles and Zoe are the only European nationals living in Rose Hill. Madame Crystal affects a Hungarian accent, but she was born in and lived most her life in Chicago. So this leaves only Charles and Zoe. Who else could attract the presence of two agents such as yourselves. Moreover, the French couple is relatively new to the village, and they really stand out here.

ELISE
They do? How so?

ARTHUR

So, I'm correct.

ELISE

Yes. You are correct; for the most part. This saves us time. How are they out of place, Arthur?

ARTHUR

They are too normal. In any other town in America they would blend in, particularly in the larger towns, but here they are unusual. I find them polite, quiet, and unpretentious. If you policed this town, you would fnd that odd, very welcome I must say, but still odd.

RENO

That is really all that we have on them as well. What can you tell us about Rose Hill? Maybe our knowing the village will provide insight into these new arrivals.

ARTHUR

Sure. If you are not going to have any goldwasser, Would you like some coffee? (*no thanks*)

Well, where to start? Rose Hill is a village, about 300 inhabitants more or less. Thousands of tourists of course, especially in season. You probably aren't interested in the tourists; most of them are day trippers passing by on the Interstate. That is what I thought you two were. The tourists look like anyone. Although Elise, you're more attractive than most.(*pause*) I say that only as a seasoned and trained observer of faces.

ELISE

Of course, I understand.

ARTHUR

As to the permanent residents, most of them live by this tourist trade. We have a couple of dozen psychics, a couple of diners, some gift shops, 3, no 4 bed and breakfasts. That's about it for Rose Hill itself. The rest of the folks are into hunting, fishing, and logging. The locals call this region God's Country.

ELISE

You yourself are not local, Arthur?

ARTHUR

No, I spent most of my career doing big city policing, before taking this job. I'm semi-retired. As I was saying, the locals call this area God's Country, although there is a contingent that considers Rose Hill the Devil's corner.

RENO

Is that why Rose Hill has a police department?

ARTHUR

We don't.

RENO

But you're the sheriff of it.

ARTHUR

I sure am. In fact, I'm the entire department. Except for the town council, who are all sworn deputies. But that was just for Federal grants.

RENO

Federal grants?

ARTHUR

Of course, you should be familiar with them. Heck, there is so much money floating around to fight this war on whatever and that war on something else. We, the « deputies » and me, we take turns going to conferences on the latest police tactics, and the shows, especially if they are somewhere warm. Or somewhere fun. I'd really like to go back to New York again, they have some of the best Fusion restaurants.

ELISE

So, do you like Fusion restaurants, Arthur?

ARTHUR

You bet. Who doesn't? I suggested to Eddie, who owns Eddie's diner that he needed to think about some fusion cuisine. His reaction made it clear that he was thinking of nuclear fusion. I dropped it.

RENO

So you have a police department in order to acquire Federal police grants and attend conferences?

ARTHUR

That is a part of it.

RENO

It sounds as if that is the biggest part of it. I noticed that you are not even carrying a firearm.

ARTHUR

You're not very observant for an agent Reno. It's in my pocket. Low profile policing. It comes highly recommended for law enforcement in towns and villages such as mine.

ELISE

Really? (*looks at Reno*) You have heard of this?

ARTHUR

Apparently he hasn't Elise. (*to Reno*). We learned this in one of the conferences. I think it was in Miami, 4 years ago. Now, Miami, they certainly give New York some competition.

RENO

In conferences, I'd have thought Orlando, not Miami.

ARTHUR

No, not conferences. In Fusion restaurants. So, anyway, I am a real cop, I carry a real gun, and I stay up to date on all of the police stuff.

RENO

Police stuff? Low profile policing, guns in your pocket. Are you serious?

ARTHUR
Totally. Do you see how shiny my badge is? That was recommended also, in the same lecture, if I remember correctly. See Elise, I work mainly with locals and tourists. Its sad, but very few people today respect what I do. What we do. The only ones who seem to respect the law, ironically, are the drunks.

Maybe the alcohol makes them nostalgic. That's why the badge is so shiny; it is designed to attract their eyes, to incite nostalgia in them and make them more docile. It works for me.

You really should attend some of these conferences, Reno. Elise, how about Interpol, surely they are enlightened, being European and all.

ELISE
Of course, Arthur. What you are saying makes a great deal of sense. Perhaps you could come to Europe sometime to share with us your knowledge.

ARTHUR
You are from Paris?

ELISE
Yes Paris. We have many police agencies there and...

ARTHUR
Fusion restaurants. How is Paris when it comes to Fusion restaurants?

RENO
I'm sure that Paris is second to none.

ARTHUR
Elise?

ELISE
Yes, exactly. (*smiles at Reno*) Paris is second to none.

ARTHUR

Of course, there is always a naysayer.

ELISE

No, truly, Paris has many..

ARTHUR

Low profile policing.

ELISE

What? You've lost me, I don't follow.

ARTHUR

Naysayers. My son, Buck, he thinks that this low profile policing is unmanly. He even convinced the City council to take action.

RENO

(*excited*) What sort of action? Did any of it involve this French couple?

ARTHUR

Well, Buck said that since Rose Hill is a tourist attraction, that we should enhance that aspect, the aspect of the strange and the mysterious, even of danger. He said that if I were to dress in jackboots, and a Sam Browne belt, with a big gun, he has no idea how heavy those are when walking a beat...

RENO

(*surprised*): You still walk a beat?

ARTHUR

No, I don't. And I wasn't about to start. So that was his idea, me dressed up like a motorcycle cop from the 1930s. Heck, we don't even own a motorcycle. Buck suggested that we apply for a grant, but I preferred attending a conference in San Franciso.

ELISE

Fusion?

ARTHUR
Guilty as charged. But to mitigate things, a Harley is useless here in winter.
So, my son convinced the city council to hire this big time consultant from (*pronounced dew boys*) Du Bois....

ELISE
Du Bois (*French pronunciation*).   The small town about 35 kilometers west of here? I saw road signs as we drove in.

ARTHUR
Yeah. That sounds right, its over 20 miles. It's called dewboys here. Anyway this big time consultant from DuBois community college was hired by the city council. You know, I wouldn't be surprised if one of the tree spirits gave Buck the idea, Buck, I love him, but he is not that sharp.

ELISE
Arthur, I will have some of your American coffee.

ARTHUR
It's cold.

ELISE
Perfect. You did say tree spirits?   What is this term?   It is wood alcohol ?

ARTHUR
Its not jargon. Tree spirits. Spirits that live in trees. Buck, working as he does in the forest, claims to know dozens and dozens of them.   If not hundreds. He's not that swift, as I said, but he has knack for remembering names, and people seem to like him easily. So, if tree spirits exist, Buck would certainly be on good terms with them.

RENO
Even as a lumberjack?

ARTHUR

Apparently so. Some things remain inexplicable. Lets return to the case.

ELISE

Good idea.

ARTHUR

So, this consultant shows up, gives me his card, it has the letters BS after his name, so at least he's honest. He does his study...

RENO

(*impatient*) And what did he advise?

ARTHUR

Darned if I know. He prepared a beautiful paper with diagrams, color charts, footnotes, and endnotes. I read the executive summary, the introduction, the entire paper, including the so-called conclusion. I even had one of retired canines, Heimdel, sniff it.

ELISE

Arthur, I'm sure this is fascinating, but too fantastic. We have a real case to discuss.

ARTHUR

I thought that you wanted commentary on Rose Hill.

ELISE

Yes, but...

ARTHUR

So Heimdel, the retired canine, by the way he came to us courtesy of a federal grant as well, Reno....

RENO

Why did you have this Heimdel sniff the consultant's report?

ARTHUR

I was being thorough.

RENO

What did he find?

ARTHUR

Nothing at all. That was not surprising, since that was why I'd retired Heimdel in the first place; he never could find anything. But, I persisted. That is what I do.

So, next, I got the team together, that is myself and Heimdel and two of the council members. I mentioned a minute ago that they are deputized?

ELISE and RENO (*nod yes*)

ARTHUR

We decided to put some of our training to use.

ELISE

And this was training that you had acquired during these federal conferences that you attend?

ARTHUR

No, Elise. Rose Hill training. This was plan B, you might say. We held a séance. Believe it or not, you can reach your own conclusions after you stay here in town, but in my opinion the Ouija board is an underappreciated tool. So many of today's departments want to own and play with all of the high-tech gadgets. But the Ouija board functions in the dark, no batteries required. Long story short...

RENO

Short?

ARTHUR

(*to Elise*) He sure does interrupt often. Do you find that annoying?

ELISE

Yes he does. Yes I do. I'm trying to train him.

ARTHUR
Long story short, Ouija says, no keep the current uniform.

ELISE
Your retired canine, Heimdel, this dog participated in this séance?

ARTHUR
Sure, why not? He'd been through all of the training.

RENO
I'm lost. What does this epic recital have to do with our case?

ARTHUR
(more serious) You asked me for background on this village. Here it is in brief. This is a tiny town, with more than its share of kooks, fools, fakers. That extends to all levels, including the elected officials. Some folks, possibly you two would be among them, say that I am one of the freaks. Maybe, maybe not. If it helps me to do my job, to maintain peace in Rose Hill, then I will use it. Whatever it takes.

And then there are the tourists, tens of thousands of whom descend on Rose Hill. Most are harmless and ordinary looking, many of them are in pain, in anguish, and searching relief. And some tourists are just as freaky as the psychics that they come to see.

There is some bad blood between Madame Crystal, a psychic with the fake Hungarian accent, and many of the other women in town, Zoe included. Probably due to the shortage of sane men around here, although other locals might attribute it to bad energy.

Everything has to be considered in the realm of what may loosely be called magic.

ELISE
So this « magic » is like a constant force of gravity. It is always there, inescapable.

ARTHUR

Absolutely.   Well said.   I'll use that turn of phrase in the future.
Thanks, Elise.

RENO

How are you able to function? Not knowing which is true and what is
false? So many lies.

ARTHUR

You've been an agent for how many years?

RENO

Over a decade, why do you ask ?

ARTHUR

Everyone lies. Surely you've discovered that, after 10 years in law
enforcement. Here, in Rose Hill, just replace lies with imaginings. That
helps. I used to receive so many calls reporting crimes that would occur in
the future. The vast majority of these alleged crimes would have been
outside of my jurisdiction even if they had actually occurred. I don't police
the entire planet.

So I gave a special phone number to the chronic callers, and I listen to
their recorded messages once a week or so. I don't have time, you can see
how busy I am here, to chase phantoms. And I mean literal phantoms. I
have real duties to execute.

ELISE

Such as?

ARTHUR

My main duty is maintaining the peace, as I said. In Rose Hill, that
entails keeping the peace between the charlatans and the tellers. These are
two camps, common in most small towns, with skirmishes, betrayals,
crossovers, all of the drama of a chess match.

RENO

If you like chess. Arthur, as you said this happens in all towns. Its
human nature. People use sex, money, prestige to keep score.

ELISE

And as motivators. Even without these, people would still compete. They would still lie, cheat, steal. Just for the thrill, just because it is something to do.

ARTHUR

Elise, you are hard for someone so young.

ELISE

(*slips up due to fatigue*) 50 murders will do that.

ARTHUR

Charles? 50 murders? You must be mistaken.

RENO

We don't know. I can tell you that the bureau has no evidence that either Charles or his companion Zoe has committed any crime whatsoever.

ARTHUR

And yet I see the FBI and Interpol before me, in a town that hasn't had a murder in... I can't remember. It was long before my arrival here. I'm positive about that.

ELISE

Arthur, who are these tellers that you mentioned, a rich, powerful family?

ARTHUR

No, sorry to confuse you. It is my shorthand for whatever it is that these folks think they are. Soothsayers, mystics, mediums, psychics, shamans. I lump them all together under the term tellers. The tellers seem to have some authenticity, some true sense, whereas the charlatans have none. The charlatans, the fakers, are like reporters or opinion writers, claiming to have secret knowledge or secret sources from the great beyond. Just fake news in my opinion.

ELISE

How do you distinguish the fakes from these tellers?

RENO

(*excited*) Yes, how?

ARTHUR

(*chuckles*) Well, I'm not psychic. I rely on the three C's.

RENO

Oh?

ARTHUR

Not O, C's.   Lighten up Reno, this is a conversation between three highly trained law enforcement professionals, not one of Madame Crystal's séances. Some banter helps.

ELISE

You've mentioned this Madame Crystal several times. Is she a medium?

ARTHUR

She is not a medium, but a psychic. These tellers are very particular about distinctions. All mediums are pyschics but not all psychics are mediums. Just as all heart surgeons are doctors, but not all doctors are heart sugeons.

ELISE

Thanks for the clarification, Arthur. So, this Madame Crystal, this psychic, she is one of the tellers?

ARTHUR

Cris?   Sure. She's a teller. She's also a looker. Unfortunately, she's not a keeper. There are some outlet malls over near DuBois. They sell all the big name brands, they might even carry Gucci.   I've not been there myself. But all of the items on sale there are seconds, marred or damaged in some way.   Good enough for some folks, but not for the discerning customer. Your bag, it is first rate, correct?

ELISE

Yes, of course. I know what you mean.

RENO

I don't.   Are we going shopping?   Maybe I would follow this conversation between professionals better if you two spoke in French.

ELISE

Arthur means that Crystal is somehow damaged. Correct?

ARTHUR

Correct. She is a good teller, but definitely not a keeper. But I digress. The three C's: cost, clothes, and chimes.

This is my checklist. If the clothes are normal, at least Rose Hill normal, and the cost is low, and there aren't any chimes, then this is likely a teller.

Unfortunately, some of the charlatans try to copy this style, but their greed usually gives them away. At the same time, some of the tellers realize that many of their clients want the movie experience, so that they have to dress the part.   Many of these tellers keep a veritable wardrobe of « costumes ».   At first this might resemble a call girl accommodating fetishes.

RENO

It sure does. Lies overlaid on lies.

ARTHUR

And there you would be wrong. They do it for the benefit of the client. Just like a priest wearing colorful robes and using incense on special days. It helps bring peace to these clients. Many of them are in pain.

RENO

So whether you or I believe it Arthur, you're stating that the tellers are providing a real benefit to their clients?

ARTHUR

If not a benefit, at least a service that the client values. I've spoken enough. What are your plans? Do you need any other assistance from me?

RENO

I am not sure if we do or don't, Arthur. Elise is running this portion of the operation.

ARTHUR

Operation?

RENO

Inquiry, investigation. The word operation may overstate the situation.

ARTHUR

Ok, Reno. The FBI certainly has a large vocabulary. Elise what do you consider this to be? Does 50 murders make it inquiry? That's enquette in French if I recall. Or an operation?

ELISE

Does it matter what we call it? You obviously studied French, Arthur. How about Shakespeare. « A rose by any other name ». Reno will speak with Charles and Zoe tomorrow, using some information that I can't share with you. He will not represent himself as a special agent.

RENO

It's called reconnaissance Arthur.

ARTHUR

That sounds very much like low profile policing, Reno. See Elise, even the FBI can appreciate new techniques.

RENO

(*sighs*) Based on my findings from this low level policing, I have no clue as to what they may be, Elise will pay them a second call, also undercover.

ARTHUR

Its a shame that you can't take Heimdel with you, but Charles would recognize him for sure. Everyone knows Heimdel.

ELISE

Arthur, it's evident that you are not the country rustic that you seek to portray. Reno and I will be here only a day or so, and then you can return to your normal life, such as it is in Rose Hill.

ARTHUR

I hope that I've given you some useful information. I have a few records in the back that might assist you as well. If you wait here, I will go run copies of them for you. (*exits stage left*)

RENO

Wow! That was beyond bizarre. This village is... I can't think of a word that accurately describes it. And all of these coincidences: the French speaking Sheriff, the son Buck....even that special phone number that Arthur mentioned for crank calls.

ELISE

I've come too far to stop because of these coincidences. They might even be construed as supporting evidence that we are on the right track here in Rose Hill. Reno, you must perform to your best with Charles tomorrow. Practice your lines tonight like a real actor.

RENO

Therein lies the problem, Elise. I don't have any lines, you're expecting me to improvise everything. This is a blind audition, not a performance. Worse, if this seer of a sheriff alerts Charles, we may see his acting ability tomorrow as well.

ELISE

Whose, Charles'?

RENO

Yes. We've already seen quite the Sheriff put on quite a show, haven't we?

ELISE

Indeed. This could become very dangerous if Arthur is part of Charles' syndicate.

RENO

No kidding! But all of this is premised on a few slips of paper. It may develop into nothing.   Zero plus zero still equals zero.

MC

(*enters, ignoring closed sign*)   Good afternoon.

RENO

Hello,   I think that the office is closed.

MC

Is the sheriff in the back office? I'll just wait.

ELISE

Yes, he should return very soon.

MC

Vous-êtes Française?

ELISE

(*startled*) Oui. It seems that quite a few people speak French here, even Ar, even Sheriff Arthur.

MC

Spirits speak in many languages, including French. Just earlier today, I spoke with a québécoise outside…

ELISE

Of Charles' house?

MC

Yes, how did you ever guess that ? Are you a friend of his as well?

ELISE

No, not really. He and I had common interests, here and in France. I was given his address and…

MC

(*suspicious*) So you are here for a reading?

ELISE

Charles is a psychic, Mrs….?

MC

Madame Crystal. No. Charles is not a psychic. If he were, he would have discarded his unfaithful girlfriend by now.

ELISE

He has a girlfriend in town? I thought that he would still live alone?

MC

Oh yes, a very pretty, and young, French girl. She is the psychic.

(*Elise and Reno exchange a glance. Door opens and Arthur enters stage left, sees MC, pauses*):

ARTHUR

Here you go folks. Enjoy your stay.

RENO

Thanks Sheriff. Bye now. (*Elise and Reno exiting stage right*). Goodbye Madame Crystal. (*exit stage right*)

MC

What did they want?

ARTHUR

Typical tourists. They wanted my recommendation on which psychic to see. They thought that I could provide the name of a credible one. I keep a list of those ones handy so that the tourists always leave satisfied.

MC

So they will come to see me. I'm credible. (*pause*) This town is full of frauds.

ARTHUR

And worse.

MC

Worse?

ARTHUR

Rose Hill has the usual array of failings, misdeeds, and sins. Those two tourists may or may not visit you for a reading. (*laughs at MC's expression*). I give them the same list that is distributed at the tourist office, I just randomize the order.

I can't play favorites, not even with my favorite. (*Arthur embraces and kisses MC, who is receptive. Arthur then guides MC to stage right door*)

Look Cris, I have some more work to do. I'll stop by to pick you up at 7. I could really go for some Hungarian goulash tonight.

MC

For dinner?

ARTHUR

Not for dinner. For dessert. (*another kiss and then MC exits. Arthur verifies that closed sign still in place and this time locks the door*).

(*Walks to back bookcase, retrieves hidden tape recorder and walks to desk. Sits down, pours another glass of Goldwasser*)

Some folks in town swear by Houdini and Ouija, I prefer Sony. (*presses button and hears voices of Elise and Reno*)

ACT I

SCENE 3 the next day, mid-morning

> (*Charles and Zoe's residence doorbell rings*)

CHARLES

Hello. Who are you?

RENO

Hi. I'm Reno. Are you Charles?

CHARLES

Yes.

RENO

I'm here to see you about an ad. Several in fact.

CHARLES

Reno, you said? Are you the one that called earlier?

RENO

No, it wasn't me. So, about these ads, they are yours?

CHARLES

Come on in Reno, have a seat. Can you show me this ad?

RENO

(*passes 2 or 3 to Charles*) Here, these are some that interest me.

CHARLES

They do, in what way? Are you looking to apply for this one, or this one?

I'm not sure why you have come here. I'm not looking to hire anyone, I'm thinking of retiring myself. These are not my ads.

CENTER>RENO</CENTER>

RENO

These aren't your ads?

CHARLES

Certainly not. I notice that these are all from the New York Journal. I subscribe to that, but I have never placed an advertisement with them. Why did you come to my house? My address is not listed in any of these clippings.

RENO

I saw these ads, and called about this one, it seemed a better fit than the others. They asked me some strange questions and then, once they were satisfied with my answers, I was given your name along with the name of this town. They also told me that you had a French accent.

CHARLES

Oh, those people. I work with them periodically. I see their ads now and again, and they send candidates to me from time to time. I perform a small service for them, really for the candidates, candidates such as yourself.

RENO

Hmm, I'm confused as what this is all about. I thought that this was a simple whack..

CHARLES

We don't use words like that here. Wacky can be interpreted as an insult.

RENO

I wasn't going to say wacky, but.....

CHARLES

Peu importe. Never mind. So, as I was saying, we perform this service on behalf of the organization that posted this ad, and in return they obtain a more complete picture of you, more in depth information on your qualifications. You sit with my consultant for an hour or less, she will ask questions, really you just tell us whatever you want to share, and we confirm your account with one or more third parties. After that, if the stories correspond, I will be comfortable in notifying the poster of the ad that you are an honest person and might be a good fit for the work that they need done.

RENO
Questions, confirming accounts, third parties?   What are you, an attorney? I'm not a snitch.

CHARLES
No, I am not an attorney, and I don't believe that you are a snitch.
(*calls to Zoe*): Zoe, are you ready?

ZOE
(*enters stage left*) Hello.

RENO
Oh, hi.

CHARLES
Have a seat, Reno.   Please sit here, across from Zoe, she's my consultant. (*dims light a bit*) That's better.

RENO
I don't like this. What is this, hypnosis? I told you that I am not a snitch. And I am not a freak either, I saw all of the weird shops up and down the street. This place gives me the creeps.

CHARLES
Reno, you are not a snitch and you are not a freak. Neither are we, at least we both aren't. So what are you Reno?

RENO
Like the guy said on the phone before, he told me your name....

CHARLES
I doubt very much he said anything specific, other than my name and that of Rose Hill. He may have implied, or led you to believe something...

RENO

Yeah, that's right. He was very cagey, just like you. Hey, was that you?

CHARLES

No, it wasn't me. I have no idea who it was. So what are you Reno? (*pause*) There is no reason to say it directly, we'll get there. So, let's begin. Zoe will simply ask you some questions, nothing is being written down or recorded.

ZOE

Hello again, Reno.

RENO

(*still nervous, but attracted to Zoe*) Hi., again. I like your accent.

ZOE

You mentioned all of the strange shops, up and down the street.

RENO

Yeah. It's creepy.

ZOE

Hocus pocus and magic, and creepy things like that?

RENO

Yeah, all of that.

ZOE

Psychics and mystics. Maybe some witches? Did you see any witches, Reno ?

RENO

(*looks at Charles, starts to rise*) Look, I may have the wrong house. I drove straight here from Detroit.

CHARLES

You may leave at any time Reno. Our time is valuable. We have other candidates coming.

RENO

The caller you mentioned?

CHARLES

No, there was no caller. That was just a simple test to see if you'd lie immediately. See, I am being honest with you. We will have other candidates, these ads reach a national, well, really an international audience. That is the idea. You're nervous, frightened...

RENO

No I'm not. I just don't like all this spooky business.

CHARLES

You're confused, hesitant. It's normal. Zoe is not a witch.

ZOE

No, I am just a fun-loving medium.

RENO

(*laughs despite himself*) Fun-loving medium. (*A bit flirtatious*) What is that? What type of fun ?

ZOE

I'm not sure. I only said it to help you relax.

RENO

(*disappointed*) Oh.

ZOE

But I am a medium. Relax Reno, I don't bite, I don't issue curses. So let me ask you, what is a medium? In your own words.

RENO

A medium, why that is omeone who casts spells, and talks to the dead, and predicts the future.

ZOE

Voila. That is what many people think. That is quite a skillset for one person, Reno. I am afraid that I can't live up to so many expectations. All that I do is talk to the dead.

RENO

(*jumps*) We're getting creepy again.

ZOE

(*smiles*) Sorry Reno, takes his hand (*Reno starts but does not withdraw his hand*). I try not to be creepy, but sometimes I can't help it. (*pause*) I should be clearer, I talk with the dead. Anyone can talk to them, including you Reno. You could talk to the deceased if you wanted to, couldn't you?

RENO

Uh, sure. I don't see why not, its a free country.

ZOE

Ok. So you might talk to a deceased relative of yours, but they don't respond to you. Did they?

RENO

(*jokingly and then more serious*)   Not recently. No, not at all.

ZOE

You mentioned that you drove here, correct?

RENO

Yes. It was a vey long drive.

ZOE

Did you listen to the radio along the way? Some music, and news?

RENO

Sure. But the reception was not very good, you really live in the middle of the sticks.

ZOE

The reception is always excellent for me. And did you speak on the CB radio, Reno?

RENO

CB radio? No. The car doesn't have one, it's a rental.

ZOE

So, don't you see the parallel? That is the difference between you and me, Reno. I have a CB radio, so that I have two way communication, whereas you only have one way communication. Not magic, not creepy.

RENO

I don't know. Not so much, but still creepy.

ZOE

So what I need to do, what you need to do in order to be considered for hiring, is to let us talk to some of your acquaintances who can vouch for your CV.

RENO

My what?

ZOE

Sorry. Your resume, your work history.

RENO

That's it? I drove all the way here to this middle of nowhere, just to have you make a few calls?

CHARLES

They are very long distance calls.

RENO

I expected to have an in person interview with a classy outfit. I've landed instead in this town which resembles a county fair.

CHARLES

The fair is next week. We're still decorating for it.

ZOE

Shhh Charles. You know that your presence during the sessions can be disruptive. If you must remain, please be silent.

Yes, Reno, very long distance calls. We need to speak to some of your late acquaintances.

RENO

You want to speak to some of my dead friends? Good luck with that.

ZOE

I have all sorts of luck. No Reno, not friends, but folks who would not consider you to be friendly at all. Someone with whom you may have had business. Someone who can and will corroborate that you and he *(pause)*, or she, parted on bad, very bad terms. So bad in fact, that the terms of that separation would prove that you are wonderful match for one of these ads.

RENO

Can we take a break for a minute? I'm am still trying to understand this.

ZOE

As you wish. *(stands and exits stage left)*.

RENO

(stands and approaches Charles) Is she serious?

CHARLES

Yes. Here, have a glass of water.

RENO

Yes? Just yes?

CHARLES

Yes should be sufficient. Zoe has told you everything that you must know in order for her to complete your background check.

ENO

Background check? She started talking about dead people and radios. Spooky, in a high tech sort of way And her accent is....

CHARLES

I see that you are not too flustered to have lost a sense of humor. These assignments require a cool head and often some finesse. (*sighs*)

Reno, can I call you cowboy?

RENO

Sure, it's a good codename.

CHARLES

It's not a codename. I just never met a real cowboy, and with a name like Reno, you're the closest that I've come to having done so.

RENO

Oh. I still like it a as codename.

CHARLES

Cowboy, let me tell you a make believe story, hypothetical.

There are people who, for one reason or another, would like to have their problems go away. Sometimes these problems are other people, and the resolutions can be violent, bloody. With countries, we call these wars, and before soldiers are sent to combat, they have to be in good enough health, and trained, and so forth.

RENO

Sure, I was in the military.

CHARLES

Cowboy, I don't need to know anything about you, and don't want to hear these details of your personal life. It is safer and simpler for the both of us. Let me continue. On a much smaller scale, private customers have problems too. They hire others to resolve their problems. But they need to find good employees, good specialists. And this is where we, speaking hypothetically of course...

RENO

Of course. Mais oui, I always wanted to say that.

CHARLES

Where we are found, our niche. A niche company that finds the right employee for the specific assignment. It's a boutique shop, this imaginary shop. It focuses on the personal touch, finding the right demographic.

RENO

Demographic?

CHARLES

We are approaching the 21st century, diversity is in. So, let's take your ad.

It asks for a young, athletic type, someone who can ride.

RENO

That's me. I'm very comfortable on a horse.

CHARLES

Perhaps. Why these qualities? My guess, it's just a guess, is that the client to be resolved is someone like you.

RENO

Like me? They want me to be his friend ?

CHARLES

No, well maybe yes, for a while. The client may be someone like you, or perhaps he, or she, is someone who would be comfortable with, at ease with a person such as yourself.

RENO

That seems more like a matchmaking service, rather than a...

CHARLES

Yes, it in a way it does, now that you mention it. The customer who has placed the assignment has a problem with the client. They want someone like you to resolve this client, this problem. And the reason is that the customer likes the client. They want the client to have a smooth transition. It could be a man's best friend cheating with his wife, or vice versa. It could be a single woman with a rich elderly and miserly aunt. It's a kinder, gentler, machine gun land.

RENO

(*laughs*): Neil Young. Ha! I am beginning to see. It's designed to be nonbrutal, dignified. My background is neither kind nor gentle. This way might be more fun.

CHARLES

Absolutely, cowboy. To find competent and considerate, « killers », speaking figuratively, is difficult. Aptitude and attitude, they must have both of these attributes.

RENO

And you are familiar with the customers, and targets, er, clients, and the posters?

CHARLES

I know nothing of any of them. This is just a story. Fictional. But in this fictional world, I would still know nothing. I am only a link, loosely connected. I provide nothing more than a background check. There is no reason for me to know who the client is, who the customer is, who you are for that matter. It's immaterial.

RENO

That makes sense. So, for this process to move forward, I need to pass the background check. Zoe conducts it?

CHARLES

That is correct. Are you ready, cowboy?

RENO

Lets mount up, Charles. Cowboy is ready.

CHARLES

(*walks stage left to call to Zoe*):   Zoe, we can start again if you are
ready.

ZOE

(*sits and takes Reno's hand, who does not jump this time*):   Hello yet
again Reno. Relaxed?

RENO

Yes, I'm fine.

ZOE

Bon. So, are you able to think of a person that fits the description that
you and Charles discussed?

RENO

Well there are a few, but I am not sure that they would know my name.
That was the entire idea, I thought, to be incognito.

ZOE

Not for our purposes. We need a witness, someone you can alibi you, so
to speak. Someone who can convince us that you are guilty.

RENO

I've always found an alibi to show my innocence, not my guilt.

ZOE

You've never seen me before. Candidates often proclaim their guilt
here. Often, their alibis and their confessed guilt melt here with me, and
with them.

RENO

Them?

ZOE

The dead. Is there someone that I can contact for you? A name? A date? A location?

RENO

Well there was a Wilson Purcell. About 4 years ago, on Lake Superior. June, I think, no, it was July. Does this help?

ZOE

Four years ago? I need something more recent. On the other side, the spirits seem to lose interest in the world that they've left behind. After 6 months or so, they seem to have truly moved on. Their deuil, sorry, they mourn, just as we do. They seem to go through the same stages as us.

RENO

You certainly seem well versed in this….this….

ZOE

Yes. (*sadly*) It's all that I do.

RENO

So more recent than 6 months? I can do that, let me think for a minute.

ZOE

That would be ideal. Some of the more introverted spirits can remain in what I call a connectable state for years, but their testimony becomes suspect. It begins to blur, they conflate events, exaggerate. They forget the true us and they also forget the true them.

RENO

That sounds like some of my old high school buddies.

ZOE

Good, Reno, you are relaxed. So let's see if we can find someone.

ACT I

SCENE 4 a few hours later

(*Charles and Zoe's residence, both are eating*)

CHARLES

Well?

ZOE

Il se prend pour Jean Reno.

CHARLES

A fake?

ZOE

Possibly. He certainly has knowledge of many murders, quite a variety in technique. Either he is as good as he claims, and no one ever recognized him, or he was just an assistant.

CHARLES

What about police? Could he be police?

ZOE

I can never tell. I'm not psychic in that way. What did I say to Reno? I'm just a fun loving medium.

CHARLES

So he could be police?

ZOE

Does it matter? He failed the test. Your test.

CHARLES
Yes, you're right. The test is foolproof.

ZOE
All of the spirit references who were able to make an identity selected someone else. I know these ghosts, Charles. Some of them will talk and talk and talk just to remain in contact with this side. They try to play psychic from the over there. One was very persistent, he wanted me to tell him who I had in front of me. He just did not want to give someone else a chance to speak.

CHARLES
Are you able to see them, these spirits?

ZOE
Sometimes. It's more like a montage of photos, interspersed with film clips.

CHARLES
A kaleidoscope of images?

ZOE
That describes it. Somewhat.

(*doorbell rings*)

ELISE
Hi, I'm Elise, have I come at a bad time?

CHARLES
(*smiles/flirting*) That depends. What are you here for? Not to save my soul, I hope?

ELISE
You must be Charles, I recognize your French accent. I've come to see you about the ad.

ACT I

SCENE 5   30 minutes later

(*Madame Crytal's reading room, various signs, such as RIP means do not disturb, life is for the living, your only choice is to get over it, I help the living, and the dead are beyond needing assistance, they have their own club*)

(*Photos of well known, powerful men and women, all living in 1992. Donation box, with price of $30. I'm a psychic, not a medium*)

RENO
(*enters stage left*)   Hello Madame Crystal, we met yesterday.   I've come to see if you have time to do a reading.

MC
We did? Yesterday? I'm sorry but I don't recall. This is a very busy time of year, I read for so many clients and meet so many folks each day during high season.

RENO
I can see that, the parking lot is filled to overflowing. Are you free now?

MC
You're in luck, yes I'm available. We weren't properly introduced yesterday, and for my new clients, such as yourself, I'll refer to you simply as John. If we continue to see each other, you may disclose your true name to me. Or not. It will be your choice.

RENO
OK, Madame Crystal.

MC

Good, I prefer that, or simply Madame. Please have a seat and relax. (*Reno sits*)

RENO

I see that you are a psychic and not a medium, Madame Crystal. What is the difference?

MC

In my case, it means that I don't deal with dead issues, particularly the dead themselves. I've no talent in that area, nor any interest. If you are here to talk with a passed over relative or loved one, I can't help you.

RENO

I'm not. Do you have many folks that want that?

MC

Yes, too many. This is why I have the signs that you see. The mediums garner all the publicity and for what? The only advice that they can give to their clients is to move on, to get over it. The dead are dead. They can be incredibly tedious. Many of these dead souls complain, or forget, or refuse to respond to calls during readings; I think that those ones have moved on themselves. The client may need time to grieve, but that does not change the outcome. In my opinion, rest in peace means do not disturb.

RENO

I see what you you're saying. But since you are not a medium, how do you know so much about the dead?

MC

This is high season, but in the winter, it can be very dead, sorry for the pun, in Rose Hill. We share stories and experiences. The mediums really like to brag. I do so much more for my clients than they do for theirs. But who brags about it? Them. Not me.

RENO

So you focus on the living, the here and now?

MC

And what may come. Essentially, I determine what your body, and the energy fields around you have to tell me about your nature, your psychic history, and how that can determine which decision path may or may not be appropriate for you. Its similar to a lie detector, but that oversimplifies it.

RENO

So, I can't lie to you and get away with it?

MC

You might, but that is not important.

RENO

That's good, but I have nothing to hide.

MC

(*pauses for effect*) John, we all have something to hide, if not from others, then from ourselves.

RENO

Interesting.

MC

If you like, I can help you with life choices, career, love, et cetera, or more generally with what may not be a good choice, seeing something in your energy that you probably can't. So, shall we proceed? If so, that will be $30. Have you visited a psychic before, John?

RENO

No, not really. I'm not really sure why I'm here. Curiosity, I imagine.

MC

Curiosity is not unusual. It's a cold reading. (*pause*) Since you have no prior experience, this process may not seem different, just odd. Just relax and be natural, you don't have to think of anything, or do anything in particular. (*MC stands and walks around Reno. Stops to touch his hair, sniffs him, places hands near his shoulders, near his chest, then places one hand on back and chest simultaneously, then places hands a few inches away from head, chest, shoulders, as if measuring the heat from a campfire from various diirections and varying distances. This can take a minute or so. Then returns to seat*) It may seem odd, but science advances every day. There are PHds in pyshics searching for neutrinos, and no one considers them weird. What I do is science as well, not everyone understands this.

RENO

I never thought of it that way before.

MC

You are much darker than I would have at first surmised. You've spent a large amount of time in, or near the dark side.

RENO

Well, I did attend and finish law school. But since then…

MC

That explains it. I've seen this before in other clients.

RENO

You're joking Madame.

MC

Only truth is funny, John. You have dark spots, and cold spots that are like psychic scars. Your energy cloud has a great deal of turbulence. You've had some bad experiences. Some of them are like tattoos, self inflicted scars or markings, the result of poor choices.

RENO

I do? What does that tell you ?

MC

Typically this happens when someone hovers around their true nature, without surrendering themselves to it. As an attorney, you are attracted to the criminals that you defend, their lifestyle. You enjoy the proximity to criminality. You resemble a vampire, an emotional vampire, where illicit activity is like nourishment. You require criminality as much as you require food.

RENO

Me? A criminal?

MC

Not a criminal per se, but you live as one vicariously through your clients. A sports fan is a more pleasant analogy; you both like the thrill without real risk.

RENO

Are you suggesting that I abandon the law and become a criminal?

MC

No. I would advise you to do anything except that. Do not abandon your career. It keeps you satiated, and safe. Without the law, you would be a criminal. We have enough of those.

RENO

Criminals or attorneys?

MC

Both. In your case, it is close to being the same animal. Fortunately, you will outgrow this.

RENO

I will? When?

MC

Oh, not for many years. It is like an addiction, correction, like an allergy that children outgrow as they reach physical maturity. Likewise, our spirit peaks and then weakens over our lifespan. The pleasant memories of evil will be enough to sustain you.

RENO

Evil?   Pleasant memories of evil?   This is quite a provocative conclusion from, what did you call it, a cold reading? All of this is dervived from energy clouds that surround me?

MC

Yes. Does a doctor use much more equipment in performing a quick medical examination? I know my business just as well as a doctor knows his. Or hers. It comes from experience, the same as in any profession.

RENO

But evil? Evil is over the top, don't you agree ?

MC

Let's compromise and refer to them as fantasies, dark fantasies.

RENO

Everyone has fantasies, Madame Crystal.

MC

Very good, John. You are beginning to see and accept a truth that you have denied to yourself, John. Even one event can tip your life's direction. Fantasy can bleed into reality.

RENO

Hmmm.   So while I am wating for my psychopathic tendencies to atrophy, what do you suggest?

MC

Acting.

RENO

Acting how?

MC

Stage acting. Try for roles that are the most villainous, they will help you act on these fantasies is a safe manner.

RENO

I like that idea. I've acted before, I could do so again. Its amazing how you have such great advice for me after only a few minutes.

MC

Of course it is, you came to Rose Hill for a reason. You are receptive to advice now, as you were not in the past. (*pause*). I am pleased that you accept this. Now for the bad news.

RENO

Up to now, this has only been good news? (*pause*) What can possibly remain with which you will be able to disappoint me?

MC

You are a loner. In another century, you could have been a cowboy, or a gunslinger. Remain a loner.

RENO

That's it?

MC

Yes. This leads invariablely to a solitary existence. A permanent single. This is simple at your age, you may still envision it as your normal state, even fun and desirable. But it will become more difficult, and then unbearable, even a few short years from today. You must never marry, nor have children, as that will bring no one, including yourself, any happiness.

RENO

You have given me quite a diagnosis, Madame Crystal. I will certainly need to reflect on your findings. Its not quite what I expected.

MC

Rose Hill has that effect, John.

ACT I

SCENE 6

(*Charles and Zoe's residence, the same time as scene 5*)

ZOE

And now, what I need from you Elise, is a name, a date, a location. Something recent would function best.

ELISE

Recent? Oh, that would be Guy Lenoir, my late uncle, 4 days ago, in Prigny. That's in France, of course. It's a village near Fountainbleau. Will that suffice?

ZOE

Four days ago, that is recent. (*takes Elise's hand*). Let's try to contact him, Elise.

ELISE

Being a medium is this easy?

ZOE

For me it is. I am very good at what I do. Let's see if you are just as good at what you do. (*closes eyes*) Guy, Guy Lenoir, can you hear me?

ELISE

(*whispers*) He doesn't, didn't speak much English.

ZOE

(*reopens eyes*) Ca ne fait rien. Most of our candidates only speak English. It is a bad habit that I've acquired. They expect me to speak aloud, I don't need to but it seems to keep the candidates from growing figidy. They are spooked, sorry, no pun intended, more by silence than by the anything else. (*closes eyes again*).

ELISE

I'm calm. I am not the fidgety type.

ZOE

Guy Lenoir.   Guy Lenoir.

No, not you.   No, not now. It's no use, I cannot be with you, later, yes, I promise.

Guy Lenoir.   Guy Lenoir.

Bonjour Guy. Un moment, s'il vous plait.

(*opens eyes*) I have him now, Elise   (*releases Elise's hand*).   I will connect with him for a few minutes. You're free to stand and stretch if you like. (*recloses eyes*).
(*Elise stands, stretches, and walks around the small room, looks at photos, sees Charles doing a puzzle in the newspaper.   During this time, Zoe is immobile*)

ELISE

Are you doing a crossword puzzle?

CHARLES

No, they are too difficult for me in English. I prefer Sudoku.

ELISE

Aren't they difficult as well?

CHARLES

Some are, some aren't. This one is « real killer » as they say over here. Others aren't. Just like people.

ELISE

(*smiles*) Yes, just like people.

ZOE

Adieu Guy. Merci Guy. Adieu. *(begins groaning, and slight shudders, gasps, about 30 seconds or so)*.

ELISE

(to Charles) Is this it, the contact?

CHARLES

Oh no, that has already happened.

ELISE

What are these contortions that she is having? Is she in pain ?

CHARLES

Au contraire. She enjoys it. That is just some cool down yoga. It has become quite the rage here.

ZOE

(opens eyes) Elise that was perfect. Most of your other assignments must have been less recent, less personal. It is actually easier that way, much less congestion.

(to Charles) This was less muddled than the session with Yvonne.

Elise, I am going to write my answer to the following question on this paper *(writes something and then rises and hands it to Charles)*. Elise, how did you kill Guy Lenoir ?

ELISE

(hesitates) I will write it down as well, I'd prefer not to respond aloud.

CHARLES

As you wish.

(*Elise writes something down and passes it to Charles, who opens one and reads it*)

An overdose of morphine while I was nursing him. (*Opens second*) My niece who was attending me gave me too much morphine. On purpose. (*pause*)

ELISE

Alors, c'est tout ? That's it?

ZOE

Yes. (*to Charles*) Elise has succeeded.

CHARLES

Enfin! I'll return in a minute. Elise, please wait here. (*exits stage left*)

ZOE

(*goes to stereo or other machine and plays recording of singing birds*) I like to hear songbirds, their singing keeps the voices away.

ELISE

It's very soothing. (*pause*) Which voices?

ZOE

All of them. Voices from the over there, voices from over here. Charles' voice. I sing to myself at times. Or at least I used to sing. I've grown tired of my own voice as well. It's beginning to blur with the others. I'm becoming one of them. Just another indistinct voice.

CHARLES

(*Charles enters stage left. Pauses. Walks to stereo and stops the birdsong*) I really dislike that Zoe. My mother told me once, when she was very old, that only stupid birds sing. I don't know if she believed it or if it was simply the bitterness of age expressed as anger. Regardless, she was correct, only stupid birds sing. Those are the only words of hers that I remember. (*Realizes that he has a candidate present*).

Elise, candidates arrive here often unqualified. Frequently they have no skills, no experience whatsoever. Or they were only assistants on these assignments. In fact, we had one of those earlier today.

It is refreshing to have an experienced professional join the team. I have passed on your verification.

ZOE

(*exclaims*) You've passed on the verification....

CHARLES

I have given the verification. There was no need to wait. It was as we agreed. Do you object?

ZOE

(*calmly*) No, not any longer. Turn the birds on again, please Charles.

CHARLES

In a minute, Zoe. This is a time for soaring, not for chirping. Elise, you should receive a call with details on the assignment as soon as tomorrow morning. The confirmation notice will appear in a national newspaper tomorrow (*Elise questioning look*), no, not the New York Journal, Elise, but another one. Its safer this way. When the poster of this assignment sees it, they will be certain to contact you.

This merits a glass of wine. (*walks toward wine*). Oh, zut, does your French cellular telephone work here is America?

ELISE

Yes, I tested it only yesterday. It functions without problem.

CHARLES

Perfect (*begins pouring wine*)

ELISE

Charles, you can't provide me with the details now? I'm ready to start immediately.

CHARLES

(*chuckles*) I don't have those details, Elise. I never do. Candidates, excuse me, new hires, are very anxious to know the details. Sadly, I can never satisfy their curiosity. (*raises glass*).   To Elise and a successful completion of her assignment. (*Zoe does not drink*).

Elise, let me show you some of this town. Some of it is quite bizarre.

ELISE

A qui tu le dit?

(*Charles and Elise exit stage right*).

ZOE

(*approaches photo of Eagle then returns to desk. Sits down*) Yes, Elise, you're telling me. Truly bizarre. Charles, you are so strong and confident. Such an eagle. And yet, you've just hired and toasted your own assassin. (*drinks wine and turns on birdsong*).

ACT II

SCENE 1

(*Sheriff's office*)

ARTHUR

So how goes the investigation?

RENO

Pretty well. Once Elise arrives, we can provide you with more details.

ARTHUR

That may not be necessary. I'm fairly current as to where the inquiry stands.

RENO

How's that ?

ARTHUR

I have my methods. First, yesterday, when I left you to use the bathroom, I called the FBI and then the Interpol office in Pittsburgh, it is the nearest one. Both verified your identities.

RENO

I'm esctatic to hear it that I was validated as an agent. I would have hated to find out that I was delusional. Especially about Elise. She is quite the (*pauses*) agent.

ARTHUR

She is that. (*pause*) Look at it from my perspective. Your arrival here yesterday was very unlikely. Unlikely even in the normal world. Here, it was still out of place. You would not believe the weirdoes that pass through here.

RENO

I've noticed that the weirdest among them remain and set down roots.

ARTHUR

Present company included, Reno?

RENO

(*sheepishly*) Yes, I think so. Sorry to be honest, Arthur.

ARTHUR

(*laughs*) You are probably not far wrong. I'll give you an example.

RENO

An example of being weird?

ARTHUR

I'll leave it to you to listen and decide. (*pause)* So you and Elise are who you claim to be. But that wasn't sufficient for me. The FBI and Interpol are fine references, but they did not enlighten me as to the reason for your presence here.

RENO

That's normal procedure.

ARTHUR

Undoubtedly. But this is Rose Hill, you must remember that. I have my own Rose Hill procedures here.

RENO

The goldwasser crystal ball routine, Arthur? You demonstrated that to us on Tuesday.

ARTHUR

I remember. I'm semi-retired, not semi-forgetful.

RENO

So more voices in your head, that only you can hear?

ARTHUR

Au contraire. Voices in both of our heads. (*pulls out goldwasser, shakes it and pours himself a glass*). Let me set the ambience. Reno? (*offers to pour one for Reno and then pulls it back*). Oh no, none for you, you're on duty.

RENO

Aren't you on duty also, Arthur?

ARTHUR

Always. (*takes a sip of liquer, leans over toward hidden tape recorder*) Listen carefully, you should be able to hear the voices now. (*voices of Reno and Elise heard. Look of shock on face of Reno*) (*Arthur laughs loudly*) It works every time. (*laughs*) You must have thought that I was crazy, Reno. (*laughs again*).

RENO

I still might think that you are crazy, Arthur. So, you know the true reason that bring Elise and myself to your quaint little town.

ARTHUR

That's my job; I take my job seriously. Rose Hill is my town. Its weird, that is without question. But it's mine.

RENO

You have us, sheriff.   Understand, we operate on a need to know. It's not personal.

ARTHUR

I understand that very well, Special Agent Reno. Yet I have a personal question that I'd like to pose to you.

RENO

(*laughs*) Oh, so you don't know everything.

ARTHUR

It wasn't on the tape.

RENO

Fire away, Arthur.

ARTHUR

What the heck is the story with your name? Reno, just Reno.

RENO

It's simple. Not easy, but simple is how Elise would state it. (*pause*).
My first boss in the bureau suggested to me that if I wanted to do well, that I
would need to accomplish two goals. One, I would need to make a name for
myself through hard work and positive results on important cases, and
second, it was crucial that I make myself personally memorable.

ARTHUR

That is good advice.

RENO

I thought so at the time. So, I listened to other agents, volunteered for
the difficult and important cases,.... Work, work, work.

ARTHUR

Sure. Been there, done that, still doing it.

RENO

It's normal and expected. All of the fresh agents behave in this manner.

ARTHUR

The good ones do.

RENO

That is still the majority of them, of us. So, being young and without too
much to lose, I took a risk and changed my name. I literally made a name
for myself, like an entertainer trying to distinguish himself from equally
talented competition.

ARTHUR

(*whistles*) The agency permitted you to do that? (*pause*) Clearly, they did.

RENO

It is a free country. I rolled the dice and took a chance that they wouldn't terminate me just because of that, especially given my successes in the field.

ARTHUR

Why that specific name? Why Reno?

RENO

It's reminiscent of the old West, but not readily identifiable as any one ethnic type. It could be Anglo, or Hispanic, it could even be Asian. The vagueness of the name adds to the mystery. You're not recording this, are you?

ARTHUR

There is no reason to since I'm present here in the office. Continue.

RENO

With this name, everyone envisions what they want. They have an easy time projecting with it. Heck Arthur, it even works in French, as you remarked yesterday. That was news to me.   Myth is important, even to the FBI. Sometimes it is even more important than truth.   At times, truth does not seem to matter.

ARTHUR

You know Reno, such a person could succeed here in Rose Hill.

RENO

It would be impossible to fail, I'd wager. Sorry.

ARTHUR

Full retirement is rapidly approaching for me. I might register as a psychic.

RENO

In Rose Hill? Would you be a teller or a charlatan?

ARTHUR

That depends on whether or not the batteries are working in this thing (*holding up recorder*).

RENO

As we are getting personal with each other Arthur, let me ask you a question. How did you end up in Rose Hill?

ARTHUR

Like most decisions in my life, it was by accident. Not fate as the tellers would express it. I had retired, and was going from small town to small town, doing research for a book.

RENO

A police novel?

ARTHUR

No, heck no. I'd had enough of police work, real or fictional. I was researching old stone churches in various towns, how they were built, the struggle to pay for their construction, the faith that sustained it. It was like seeing mini Americas being established throughout the state. I enjoyed the travel and the stories, but I never finished the book.

RENO

It sounds interesting.

ARTHUR

It would have been full of pictures. Books with photos sell markedly better, or so I've been told. It wasn't the money that motivated me; it was being able to capture passion in words and pictures.

RENO

You still have plenty of time to complete the book.

ARTHUR

I do, but in the process of capturing the passions of lives past, I dissipated my own. Which is why I want to retire for good, to see if it can rekindle itself.

I mentioned a job in Rose Hill to you earlier, Reno. This is not a bad place to be a one man department.

RENO

With grants and all of that.

ARTHUR

Don't scoff. It's a nice gig. I have my own network of informants, too many of course. And not enough crime about which to be informed. Your visit is the most excitement in years. But these informants, they have their value, although it can be overwhelming at times. Can you imagine being inundated with opinions and images from innumerable sources? All without any filtering. Much of it is only rumor, or deliberately misleading, sensational just to sell an agenda. Any sane person would demand that it be abolished.

But here, in Rose Hill, this is the network that keeps me abreast, even ahead of events, according to some of the more absurd informants. I call it an internet.

You'd find this network useful Reno, if you ever decide to take the job.

RENO

You can keep your so called internet, Arthur. It's not something for a sane man such as myself.

ELISE

(*enters stage right*) Good morning Reno, Arthur. Reno, I just received a call in response to the interview with Charles yesterday. Can we discuss it outside, maybe share coffee across the street at the cafe?

ARTHUR

I have coffee here, Elise. Hot or cold, your choice.

ELISE

I know, but…

RENO

He knows…

ELISE

About the coffee?

ARTHUR

About that and more.

RENO

Arthur knows everything.

ELISE

Everything?   Reno you told him everything? What type of agent are you?

RENO

The same as you. I trust my colleagues.

ELISE

(*snorts*) The same as me? Do you know the meaning of discretion?

RENO

Yes, the same as me.   Arthur recorded our conversation, our private conversation. The one that we had before we met with the Sheriff.

ELISE

(*loudly*) You can't be serious. Isn't that illegal?

ARTHUR

(*rolls his eyes*) So, what did they tell you on the phone call?

ELISE

I'm amazed that you did not wiretap my mobile phone.

ARTHUR

I don't have your number. I wouldn't do that.

ELISE

Are we being recorded now, Sheriff?

ARTHUR

The name remains Arthur, Elise. No you are not being recorded. Reno had the same question a few minutes ago.   We are all friends here. The callers what did they say?

ELISE

I was given the contract of course. Otherwise I would not have been contacted.

RENO

Congratulations!, or not (*sheepishly*)

ARTHUR

Who is the target?

ELISE

Charles. Your friend Charles.

RENO/ARTHUR

What? That can't be. No way. He must be playing with you.

ACT II

SCENE 2

(*Charles and Zoe's residence*)

CHARLES
(*getting organized for a walk, ready to leave*) Zoe, I am so happy that we have filled this opening with Elise. She's perfect, isn't she?

ZOE
In most respects, yes she is, perfect. Except for not being the first candidate. She doesn't comply with the pact that you and I made.

CHARLES
Elise doesn't fit the criteria ? She came for the interview, her credentials as a killer were validated by yourself, and she speaks French.

ZOE
She wasn't the first.

CHARLES
Sure she was. She is the first candidate since we agreed to our « pact ».

ZOE
No she isn't.

CHARLES
We've only had two, Elise and the cowboy. Reno? Cowboy is a cowgirl?

ZOE
Of course not. I was speaking of your girlfriend, Crystal.

CHARLES

My girlfriend? Zoe, I don't understand. She's not my girlfriend, you are.

ZOE

I mean your real girlfriend. What we have is…

CHARLES

Enough!

ZOE

She is a killer, your Madame Crystal.

CHARLES

Crystal, a killer? What type of sick joke is this?

ZOE

All the jokes in Rose Hill are sick Charles. Oh yes, she is a killer. I have it on very good authority.

CHARLES

From whom, your part-time boyfriend, Buck? He knows nothing about anythng in the real world.

ZOE

From her husband. Her dead husband. He appeared to me the moment that she first came sniffing around. Poison. The sign of a rookie you sneer. A rookie, but still a killer.

CHARLES

I don't know what to say.

ZOE

She also speaks French. She was a teacher of it in Chicago. You should do some background checks yourself Charles, instead of relying on me.

CHARLES

This makes no sense. She did not bring any ads, she did not mention them. It's just a coincidence. Even accepting what you say, Zoe, Elise is still the better choice.

ZOE

Have it your way Charles. I wanted to give you a chance to stop this. I need to clear my head with a walk. The birds are singing. (*exits stage right*).

CHARLES

I am going to stop this. My way. (*exits stage left and returns with portable handset*). Hello, cowboy? It's me, Charles. No, I don't have anything for you from the ads. Listen, this is really unusual for me, but I'd like to engage you for myself..... That's correct, a personal matter....... Yes, here in Rose Hill............ You could resolve it before you leave..... You would leave with and like the other tourists.... Great. Well it's two actually.... Oh the first one, you met her yesterday at my house, she held your hand.... Yes, I'm sure. I've thought for a while that things weren't working out well. I've suspected for some time. Yes, I think that it has come that, either her or I....... The second, she's another tourist in town. She is French too, she calls herself Elise. Yes, as soon as you can. Thanks cowboy.
(*returns phone stage left, returns, puts on camera, etc.*)

BUCK

(*knocks and enters stage right*) Good morning Chuck.

CHARLES

Good morning Buck. It was amazing seeing the eaglets soloing for the first time yesterday. Magnifique.

BUCK

If you feel up to attempting a longer hike today we could walk as far as Lafayette. Their grandparents have arrived.

CHARLES

Grandparents?

BUCK

Grand eagles, grandparents. I don't know which is correct. It's an older pair, the grandparents of the eaglets that intrigue you. They inhabit a large red oak. You may know it as Jefferson, the local hunters refer to that oak as Jefferson, and use it a reference point during deer season

CHARLES

But Buck, you say La Fayette. Why, is that its name? Did it tell you?

BUCK

Of course it did. The locals have a rumor that Thomas Jefferson planted trees around here, hence the name. That is ridiculous. Jefferson was never within 100 miles of what is now Rose Hill, although he would have been extremely curious about the town. But no, he was not involved.

CHARLES

Yet La Fayette was in this region?

BUCK

He was. Lafayette was a great hero of the American Revolution, a Frenchman like yourself. A count and a general.

CHARLES

A Frenchman? If you say so, Buck. Like me? I doubt it.

BUCK

It was LaFayette that nearly cut his namesake down as a sapling, but spared it, for whatever reason. Perhaps he resembled me and spoke with tree spirits.

CHARLES

I doubt that just as much Buck. Sometimes your stories are beyond…

BUCK

So my Lafayette knew your Lafayette. (*Pause*). In any case, the older eagles are in Lafayette while the young ones are in Kittana. The falcon that you spotted probably nests in...

CHARLES

Lafayette, or Karma, or Kittana. Or Godzilla. To me a tree is a tree. How on earth do you distinguish one from another? And these names that you select...

BUCK

I don't select them Chuck, I've mentioned this to you in the past. The trees tell me their names themselves.

CHARLES

So you have Buck, so you have. Grand eagles, that makes for a pleasant sound. I would have liked to have been a grand eagle, a grandparent myself. It's too late now.

BUCK

I plan on it. I will be a husband, and a father. And sometime later, there's no hurry, a grandfather.

CHARLES

Enough chirping. Lets go see this family of the treetops.

(*Charles and Buck exit stage right*).

ZOE

(*enters stage right a minute later. Doorbell rings, Elise turns to answer it, finds Madame Crystal*) Oh, it's you. Come in.

MC

Is Charles' at home?

ZOE

You have very bad timing for a psychic. (*Has a sudden thought and apologizes*):
I apologize Crystal. Please come in, would you like some tea?

MC

No, thanks. Charles....

ZOE

You must have just missed him. He was going to watch the eagles with Buck. Please, have a seat, we have something important to discuss.

MC

(*sits*) We do?

ZOE

Would you care for a cup of coffee or tea, Crystal?   I just asked you that, didn't I?

MC

Yes, you did. Is something wrong?

ZOE

Everything. Elise is in town. She stopped in to see Charles sometime recently, yesterday was it ?

MC

Elise? Who is she?

ZOE

Elise is your competition.

MC

Another psychic? Wonderful. It is just what this town needs.

ZOE

Elise is not a psychic.

MC

Then how is she my competition?   Who is this Elise?

ZOE

A very attractive woman, well dressed. Tirée à quatre épingles, you said the other day. Was it really only yesterday?

MC

It was the day before yesterday.

ZOE

Was it? The days run together like voices at a party. (*pause*) I miss parties.

MC

You must mean Yvonne, the blonde from Quebec ?

ZOE

No, not Yvonne. Elise is French, not Québécoise.

MC

I've met her Zoe, I've met Elise.

ZOE

(*alarmed*) You have?

MC

I think so, Zoe. She is certainly attractive, and very well dressed, but not as flashy as all that. She was in the sheriff's office where she was asking for a reputable list of psychics. Arthur gave her my name, of course.   So Elise can't be a psychic, unless she wanted to evaluate the competition, as you said Zoe.

ZOE

No, forget that idea. Elise is not psychic. Has she come to see you for a reading?

MC

(*perturbed, then proud*) No, not yet. But she will. (*pause*). You claim that she is my competition. I don't understand.

ZOE

She has come for Charles. She is one of his former girlfriends.

MC

That makes her your competitor, not mine.

ZOE

Not after today. I am leaving Charles.

MC

What?

ZOE

You may have him. Or you can let Elise have him. I don't care. Ca m'est égal.

MC

You decide to leave Charles the minute that Elise shows up? That's very sudden.

ZOE

I'm not doing this because of Elise, Crystal. You were correct yesterday. Too many events occurred yesterday, yes, it was yesterday, I am sure of it. It was a month compressed into a day.

MC

You are doing this because of Buck?

ZOE

Yes, Buck. (*smiles and states matter of factly*) Your psychic powers at work.

MC

You and Buck. And now this Elise swoops in to take Charles from me.

ZOE

Like an eagle.

MC

You should have left Charles months ago. You've ruined my chance at happiness, Zoe. I bet that you are ecstatic. You've always disliked me.

ZOE

I didn't dislike you Crystal. I despised you.

MC

(*rises and shouts*) I never cheated on my husband.

ZOE

(*does not flinch, laughs*) Let's not compare sins, Crystal, neither of us have the time. Yes, I used to despise you. But no more. You and Charles are a matched set. I've cleared the path for you, as much of it as I was able to clear. Only Elise remains an obstacle.

MC

(*warily*) What are you saying?

ZOE

Obstacles can be cleared. They must be cleared if you want to reach your destination. I've cleared mine; leaving Charles was the last.

MC

Cleared?

ZOE

It's a word. There are others less euphemistic.

MC

Killed? I am not a killer.

ZOE

Oh, it must be my mistake Crystal. I heard talk of poison regarding the death of your late husband.

MC

Talk, just talk. That is all that it was, or ever will be. I had my husband's remains cremated.

ZOE

The fair is next week.

MC

The fair? Next week? That's an abrupt transition. What are you talking about ? You are so jumpy today Zoe.

ZOE

Many folks around here have bonfires that week. Maybe you should light one also. Buck could bring a load of wood from the sawmill to your house. There would be no charge for a friend.

MC

(*snorts*) A friend?

ZOE

(*bites tongue*) We could be friends, or at least temporary allies. (*continues*) Without charge for a friend. The forest is filled with poisonous plants. Elise could follow in your late husband's wake. She is just a tourist, her disappearance would not even be noticed.

MC

Charles would notice her sudden absence.

ZOE

Not if you were there in her place. To fill any void.

                              MC
I don't know. (*pause*)   This is all happening so suddenly. And you and
Buck?

                              ZOE
Buck wants to marry me. I certainly won't marry Charles.

                              MC
Not even if he proposes?

                              ZOE
He won't. He's never proposed to anyone. I won't be the first woman
to marrry him, you are welcome to try your luck. Je te souhaite bonne
chance.   Trust me.
                              MC
I trust no one.

                              ZOE
(*flatly, no sarcasm*)   Then trust your psychic abilities.

                              MC
You're mocking me.

                              ZOE
No, I'm not. I am putting you to the test. Either you are psychic or you
are not.

                              MC
I am.

                              ZOE
Then trust in them, Crystal.

MC

(*thinks, then makes decision, more confident*): D'accord. You are absolutely correct Zoe. Evidently, I have misjudged you. You are more simple than I feared. You are just a weak, silly girl. French or American, male or female, there.is no difference among the weak. My late husband grew weak, too weak for me. Here in Rose Hill, the weak and silly seek me out. I need a respite from them. Charles offers that to me. You have elected to leave one of the two strong, confident men in this insane asylum for one of the weak. You are truly silly, Zoe.

There is no need for plants or firewood, or for either you or Buck to be involved. Poison is for novices. Leave the details to me, just ensure that Elise does not leave town until she leaves town permanently.

(*MC exits stage right. Afterward, Zoe exits stage left*)

ACT II

SCENE 3

(*2 hours later. doorbell rings, Zoe enters stage left to answer it. It is Elise, who steps right into the room*)

ELISE
I've come to see Charles, this is important.

ZOE
He's not here, he's hiking with a friend. He can't, won't tell you anything more. They may be back soon. You must be patient and wait for the phone call.

ELISE
I received the call earlier.

ZOE
As I feared.

ELISE
As you feared?

ZOE
(*recovering*) Yes. If you had come here without having received a call, that would show initiative and excitement. That happens from time to time. But showing up here, all flustered, that usually indicates that you have had a change of heart.

ELISE
I am not flustered. It is not in my nature to fluster.

ZOE
Would you like a cup of coffee?

ELISE

(*pacing*) Is it strong?

ZOE

Yes, it is very strong.

ELISE

Good. A cup of strong coffee would be very welcome.

ZOE

You were difficult to find, Elise. (*makes/pours coffee and adds poison in a way visible to the audience*).

ELISE

Me, I was hard to find? You were searching for me?

ZOE

I don't mean you specifically, but someone who met the criteria of the ad. They had to be French, or at least speak it, female, and a murderess. And then they had to travel to this remote village for an unknown reason to meet a total stranger.

ELISE

A great deal of this advertisement describes you.

ZOE

(*laughs*) It's only natural, as I was the one who placed the it.

ELISE

You, but why ?

ZOE

Yes. I was tired of being with Charles, with this so called life. Or at least I thought that I was. (*Approaches Elise with poisoned coffee*).

ELISE

I've come to arrest Charles, not to murder him..

ZOE

(*shocked, but still in control, sets coffee aside, out of the reach of Elise, laughs*) Arrest him? You're with the police? That can't be true. You are not even American.

ELISE

I'm an agent with Interpol.

ZOE

(*laughs again*) Since when does Interpol hire murderers? They have to hire liars of course, as everyone lies. But murderers?

ELISE

They don't. You are wondering about my reference, Guy Lenoir. This was his idea, crazy beyond imagination. But he convinced me, he convinced Interpol, he convinced the FBI that this might work. And then, Zoe, he convinced you.

It was the only way to succeed with Charles' verification process. So yes, everyone lies. Even from beyond the grave. It's disappointing to learn that the hereafter is not much different in that respect.

This lie, you accepted it.

ZOE

(*applauds slowly*)   Bravo, Elise. Bien joué . But what have you achieved? According to you, Interpol does not employ killers, but as I mentioned, they must engage liars, as everyone lies. You are not here to murder Charles, I'm overjoyed to hear that. In fact, I've changed my mind about his death.

This long search for an assassin delayed the moment when I had to choose. I know now that I could never kill Charles.

So neither of us will murder dear Charles. You've come to arrest him (*laughs*). What is the evidence? None. What is the accusation? That he held a reading in his house with a medium. What is the testimony? That the main law enforcement agent confessed to murdering her uncle and that somehow that makes Charles a criminal.
Elise, you would be ruled insane before this ever came to court.

ELISE

If you wanted to cancel the contract on Charles' life why not just do so?

ZOE

It is not that easy in this business; it is not like returning a pair of unworn shoes.

ELISE

What's done cannot be undone?

ZOE

That sounds familiar, but in this situation, it's a matter of what's not yet done cannot be undone. I can try, though.

ELISE

Does that include Charles' hiring of an assassin to eliminate you?

ZOE

(*laughs*) You are being very entertaining, Elise. What you recount is silly. It is not credible.

ELISE

As silly as your hiring someone to kill him? Charles must have realized what was happening, and saw, as I did, that the ad matches you.

ZOE

(*hesitant*) It is possible. Unlikely, but possible. Tell me more.

ELISE

It is a fact. Charles called my partner a few hours ago and gave him the contracts. Two contracts, one on you and one on me.

ZOE

I was joking before about insanity. Not now. You must truly be insane Elise. You are telling me that one of your colleagues at Interpol is on call as a murderer to hire?

ELISE

Not Interpol, he is with the FBI.

ZOE

(*laughs almost uncontrollably*)

ELISE

However, he was not able to pass your exam.

ZOE

My exam?

ELISE

Yes, only yesterday. Do you remember Reno?

ZOE

Ah, Reno. Yes, I remember now, Charles called him Cowboy.

ELISE

Charles calls him cowboy? (*laughs despite herself*) I can visualize that.

ZOE

To me he was just a frightened boy.

ELISE

He acts well.

ZOE

Not well enough it would seem. He should have worn a hat.
Regardless, he failed the exam, as you just indicated.

ELISE

He failed your exam, not Charles'. Charles hired Reno despite your
rejection.

ZOE

So Cowboy, or Reno, this G man, he will not fulfill this contract on
either you or me. It's probably not permitted in the FBI handbook. You
look ridiculous Elise, you've lost. You are performing very poorly on
today's exam. Take your zero and go back to France.

(*knock at door and Buck enters stage right, excited, sees Elise and stops
a bit short*)

BUCK

Hi Zoe.

ZOE

Hello Buck. This is Agent Elise…

ELISE

Gaar

ZOE

Elise Gaar with Interpol.

BUCK

Interpol? The police?

ZOE

Yes, the police.

BUCK

Cool. (*pause*) If this is a police matter, should my father be notified?

ELISE

Your father was notified a few days ago. This is a French matter.

BUCK

OK. So can it wait? Zoe and I have important matters to discuss.

ELISE

So do Zoe and I, and Charles. Where is Charles, Buck?

BUCK

Chuck? He is still in the woods watching the eagles. I left him there with Crystal, Madame Crystal. She said that she could give him a ride home. Zoe, Chuck told me the entire story. It was quite a surprise. He's ready to let you go. We are free to marry. He even gave his consent.

ZOE

He did?

BUCK

Yes. I drove back so quickly that I was afraid of getting a speeding ticket. It would have been worth it. Chuck said that he is going to retire from his business. To tell the truth he doesn't really appear to do much of anything. Full retirement for him.

ELISE

I doubt that very much. (*pause*) Zoe, Reno can confirm every word about these contracts.

BUCK

(*surprised*)   Do you know Reno, Agent Elise?

ELISE

(a *little embarrassed*) Just Elise is fine, Buck. Yes I know Reno. Why do you ask ?

BUCK

Chuck mentioned him as well. He asked me to call this Reno guy, is he really a cowboy, and tell him that the contracts were canceled but that Chuck would pay him anyway. Chuck is a real standup guy once you get to know him.

ELISE

You might not say that once you get to know him.

BUCK

What?

ZOE

Elise, you have nothing. And we have nothing further to discuss.

BUCK

So this French business is settled then?

ZOE

Yes, it is.

ELISE

No, it isn't.   It can't be over. There are bills remaining to be paid.

BUCK

If it is only a question about some bills due back in France, you should have just sent Zoe a letter. I know that Dad arranges these combination police/restaurant conferences, but I thought that he was unique in doing that. You came here just to collect on a few overdue bills ? I can pay them for Zoe, now that..

ELISE

They're not that sort of a debt, Buck. Charles and Zoe will need to pay them by themselves.

ZOE

It's over Elise. You failed miserably. I owe you nothing.

BUCK

This is a private matter between Zoe and me. You should leave. Now.

ELISE

No.

BUCK

So be it. I'm not going to wait any longer. Zoe, will you marry me?

ZOE

(*joyful*) Oh, yes Buck. Yes, yes, yes. (*they kiss. Suddenly Zoe falls back as if in pain*) Oh, no! Papa! Papa! No, no, no. (*collapses on chair*).

BUCK

Zoe, what's wrong. I don't understand. (*regards Elise*). Is this your doing. You should have left. Zoe, what is the matter ? This is not the reaction that I was expecting.

ZOE

(*sad*) Papa! Papa!

ELISE

Papa?

BUCK

She means Chuck. Chuck is Zoe's father.

ELISE

What? That cannot be true. We'd have known.

BUCK

No one knows. Chuck told me earlier, while the eagles were soaring. He and Zoe's mother never married and she did not identify him as the father on Zoe's birth certificate.

ELISE

Charles and Zoe have been living here as a couple. This is digusting.

BUCK

Only from the outside. It was a way for both of them to avoid entanglements. It is not what you were think, it's not that. Chuck has been protecting her, Zoe is very sensitive. But that will be my role now, as a husband, not as a father. (*Zoe recovering*) Did you hear that my darling Zoe? As a husband.

ZOE

No Buck, not as my husband, not yet. Not until after the funerals.

BUCK

Funerals? Which funerals?

ZOE

Yes. The funeral of Papa and....

(*doorbell rings, followed by Arthur and Reno hurrying in*)

ARTHUR

Good, you are all together. (*approaches Zoe*). Zoe, I have very bad news for you. I've just come from the hospital in Du Bois. There was a terrible accident up near that large tree they call Jefferson. There is another tree, an old, split oak adjacent to it.

BUCK

I left them there to come here. Madame Crystal seemed to be on a mission today. What happened?

ARTHUR

Charles and...

ZOE

(*flat, not a question*) Crystal.

ARTHUR

Yes, Crystal. They were both badly injured.

ZOE

It was Karma.

RENO

Karma? No, it was an accident.

ZOE

It was Karma.

RENO

That old oak was already damaged. And when a large gust of wind hit, the tree just buckled.

BUCK

So it was Karma after all. That is the name of that split tree, Dad.

ARTHUR

The medical team did their best, their utmost. As did Reno here. I'm sorry Zoe, but Charles is dead.

BUCK

Her father is dead?

ZOE

And Crystal.

ARTHUR

And Crystal.

ZOE

I'm sorry too Arthur.

ARTHUR

(*message sinks in*) Zoe, Charles was your father ? Is that correct? You are his daughter?

ELISE

So it would seem Arthur (*as Zoe nods yes*)

BUCK

I am so saddened for your loss Zoe, our loss. I will help with the funeral arrangements. He might like to be interred under a tree near the eagles.

RENO

He already was. (*pause*) Sorry.

BUCK

Zoe, we can discuss our wedding plans again after the service.

ARTHUR

Wedding? You and Zoe? Buck, you cannot marry Zoe. She is the furthest thing from a keeper that I can imagine.

ELISE

(*shocked at Arthur's callousness*) Arthur, now is not the time.

ARTHUR

(*deliberately misunderstands*) You are correct, Elise. Now is not the time. There is never going to be a time when she will be a keeper. Never.

BUCK

Dad, just leave. Please.

ARTHUR

Come on Reno. We are finished here (*Arthur and Reno exit stage right*)

BUCK

(*to Zoe*): Don't listen to him. What he thinks, what he said, it doesn't count. You and I do.

ZOE

He is telling the truth, Buck. It doesn't matter. Truth doesn't matter. Can you leave me now please, Buck? I need to be alone.

BUCK

Sure Zoe. I will return later. (*kisses Zoe on the forehead and exits stage right*).

ZOE

(gazes at Elise) Our business is concluded Elise. You've accomplished your mission. Charles is dead; our boutique is closed.

ELISE

You are still free. You remain a murderess, at least one by proxy.

ZOE

You have no witnesses, nothing. Take what you have and go.

ELISE

It is not enough.

ZOE

It will have to suffice.   You should thank me, Elise.

ELISE

Thank you ? For what?

ZOE

The gift that I gave you.

ELISE

Which gift?

ZOE

I gave you incontrovertible proof that your Guy lives.

ELISE

It could have been all a ruse, you are a criminal after all.

ZOE

Ten minutes ago, you were prepared to prosecute me with it, and now you reject your own evidence.   After all your efforts, both in France and here, is that what you believe? Soit. Believe what you will.

(Elise heads toward door, stage right)
Elise, may I ask you something?

ELISE

You always have more questions, don't you?

ZOE

This Guy, your so called uncle. He was your partner, yes?

ELISE

Yes, Guy was my partner at Interpol.

ZOE

But also your partner?

ELISE

(*hesitates*) Yes. (*pause*) Guy was older than me; he joked that I was young enough to be his niece. I teased him with the nickname of "Uncle".

ZOE

I don't think that they tell deliberate lies on the other side. I don't believe that they are capable of untruth in the over there. That would be too depressing to envision.

ELISE

This entire village is depressing.

ZOE

It was morphine.

ELISE

Guy had immense pain. Having cancer is like being eaten alive by an eagle.

ZOE

(*wan smile*) Being eaten alive by an eagle....I know the feeling all too well.

ELISE

Perhaps you do at that, Zoe.

ZOE

It was morphine.

ELISE

Yes.

ZOE

This is my last question, I promise. (*Pause*) If you hadn't been pursuing Charles, hadn't needed a plausible reason to act, hadn't needed a justification to kill, would you have still given Guy that overdose?

(*no response from Elise*)

Elise?

ELISE

(*pause*) I don't know. (*turns and exits stage right*)

ZOE

(*walks to retrieve the by now cold cup of coffee and sits down next to the stereo. Puts cup to her lips and sips a tiny amount*): It has gone cold. Ce ne fait rien. (*drinks most if not all of it*) I've always only known you as Charles, Papa. To me, Charles means Papa. (*pause*) So, Charles, you finally understand that you and grandmother were wrong. (*pause*) Are you certain? (*pause*) We'll listen to the songbirds together then. (*leans over and plays birdsong. As singing is heard, she leans back in chair, chin comes to rest on chest*)

FIN